TESTIMONY FROM YOUR PERFECT GIRL

ALSO BY KAUI HART HEMMINGS

TESTIMONY FROM YOUR PERFECT GIRL

KAUI HART HEMMINGS

G. P. PUTNAM'S SONS

G. P. PUTNAM'S SONS
an imprint of Penguin Random House LLC, New York

Copyright © 2019 by Kaui Hart Hemmings.
Penguin supports copyright. Copyright fuels creativity, encourages diverse voices,
promotes free speech, and creates a vibrant culture. Thank you for buying an authorized edition of
this book and for complying with copyright laws by not reproducing, scanning, or distributing
any part of it in any form without permission. You are supporting writers and allowing
Penguin to continue to publish books for every reader.

G. P. Putnam's Sons is a registered trademark of Penguin Random House LLC.

Visit us online at penguinrandomhouse.com

Library of Congress Cataloging-in-Publication Data
Names: Hemmings, Kaui Hart, author.
Title: Testimony from your perfect girl / Kaui Hart Hemmings.
Description: New York, NY: G. P. Putnam's Sons, [2019]
Summary: While their parents deal with a scandal, sixteen-year-old Annie and her brother, Jay,
spend winter break with an aunt and uncle they barely remember, uncovering family secrets.
Identifiers: LCCN 2018024212 | ISBN 9780399173615 (hardcover)
Subjects: | CYAC: Brothers and sisters—Fiction. | Scandals—Fiction. |
Secrets—Fiction. | Family life—Colorado—Fiction. | Colorado—Fiction.
Classification: LCC PZ7.1.H46 Tes 2019 | DDC [Fic]—dc23
LC record available at https://lccn.loc.gov/2018024212

Printed in the United States of America.
ISBN 9780399173615
1 3 5 7 9 10 8 6 4 2

Design by Dave Kopka. Text set in Minion Pro.

For my young adults: Eleanor, Leo, and Talcott

1

I t's an ordinary day and nothing is wrong.

I walk to my last class with this lie on repeat in my head. It's the last day before Christmas break, and I've dressed accordingly. I'm still in my conservative style—black pixie pants and an Italian wool-blend turtleneck—but for a dash of festivity I put on red plaid flats and small, antique gold chandelier earrings.

I'm pretending to be absorbed in something on my phone, but am aware of people looking at me differently, in a daring—almost gloating—kind of way. During my previous class, even Mr. Koshiba, who usually loves me for my focus and quiet enthusiasm, wouldn't look me in the eye.

Right on time, Mackenzie and her squad come around the corner, heading to Music Explorations. We exchange smiles. While I'm not in this rowdy, popular crowd, they're still friendly to me. As freshmen, they assumed we'd be friends, since all our parents are friends, especially our mothers, but they soon found I'm not like my mother or my brother. I don't like parties, I don't like to drink—I've always been too busy with ice skating—and I take school seriously. I'm like my father: ambitious.

One of the squad members—Cee—is a friend. Her dad

She takes school - very seriously

works with my father, so we hang out—mostly one-on-one. I can be dorky and relaxed with her, and vice versa. She's not with them, I notice, which is odd. I tease her for being so tethered to these girls, as if she'd float away without them.

Mackenzie looks up from her phone, and something in her expression reminds me that I'm fooling myself. It's not an ordinary day at Evergreen, and she knows it. This whole school, this whole town knows it. I lift my head a little higher, stand a little straighter.

She slows, and the other girls whoosh past like she's a rock in a river.

"Hey," she says. "Cee wanted me to give this to you." She hands me my sweatshirt that I hadn't planned on ever asking her to return. It's her favorite—a gray cashmere hoodie. I don't see why she couldn't give it to me herself.

"Is she out sick?" I adjust my saddle bag.

"Sort of," she says. I don't ask more questions, not wanting to show my confusion. "How are you doing?" she asks.

I look around. "Fine? Why?" I shouldn't have welcomed more conversation, and what is her motive for being concerned?

"Come on," she says, in a quieter voice. "I know it must be hard."

It's then that I remember. A few years ago, her mom went to jail for tax evasion, but that's hardly the same. My dad isn't guilty, and he won't go to jail. Her mom was a crook.

"It's pretty typical," I say. "In his line of work."

"Totally," she says.

Her parents were there at the opening, and I wonder if they bought in. I think back to the party where my dad announced the launch of Aria's construction. He began his speech with *I don't ask myself how much I can make. I ask myself—what can I create? What kind of life can we erect for our children?*

Afterward my grandfather, one of Genesee's founding fathers, berated him, saying that *erect* and *children* should never be said in the same sentence, but still, I could tell he was proud of my dad. Dad was following in his footsteps (or, now, the Rascal path). He was continuing the developer tradition, but stepping it up, making condo units designed like custom homes. I'd look through the dreamy and sleek artist renderings, imagining myself living there on my own one day. The building would have a gym, wine cellars, concierges, a salon, a dog park, dining rooms, a movie theater—you'd never have to go anywhere for anything. You'd live in a beautiful bubble with people just like you.

"The worst is the pity," Mackenzie says, and her face seems to tighten at a memory.

I know exactly what she's talking about. Pity is insulting, embarrassing.

"And the way you just know people will talk about you as soon as you leave," she says. "It's, like, your story. But don't worry. It wears off."

Stop reassuring me, I want to say. *Stop thinking we're the same.* Everyone at school must love this—the impeachment of royalty. I can't wait until he proves everyone wrong.

"I'm not worried," I say, tagging on a laugh. "My dad didn't commit a crime. So . . . it's not really the same."

I can tell she's offended, but I don't care.

"Tell that to Cee," she says, and walks away.

I immediately look at my phone as though it will supply an

answer. What does this have to do with Cee? Yes, our dads work together, but they're on the same side. They're in on this together. I text her:

Speak up

Something we always say when we want to hear what's what immediately, in its purest form. No BS. What's up? Speak up. Let it all out.

By the end of the day, nothing comes up or out. Maybe she was too embarrassed to come to school and face her friends, but that doesn't make sense, since she gave Mackenzie my sweatshirt to give to me. She's angry about something that I did, and now I'm mad, too. Whatever she thinks, she's got it all wrong.

2

I walk out of my bedroom to meet my dad in the living room at four thirty. Pictures of me and my brother line the hallway, black-and-white photos, all in white frames, capturing the (staged) moments in our lives. They've been taken by a professional photographer, Vincent, a man with a tropical accent who comes yearly, first week of October because a fall/winter card is classier, and barks out directions: "Tilt chin, smile, smile harder, smile not so much, jump in the air, laugh! You are so happy! You don't know I'm here!"

Yes, we're naturally wearing coordinated outfits, laughing at a hilarious joke no one told, and we don't know you're here taking pictures of our dorkdom.

When we were much younger, my brother and I enjoyed ourselves and the process. When we were laughing in the pictures, we were laughing in life. Now we stand still and grunt through various poses, then look at one another shyly afterward, as if we just participated in something lurid, which we did. We're selling people the myth of our life.

Here's my myth: I am polished, in control, above it all. I am wealthy, pretty, yet don't care about my looks or the things I have. I only have a few friends, but I'm not lonely. I'm not funny, weird, or dorky. I am Annie Tripp.

Each year Vincent is less enthusiastic as well. He knows he's complicit in the lie.

"Just grin a little so you don't look like a tiger."

"Put your arms around one another. You are brother and sister. You are family."

When we are done with our photos, our parents join in so we can take our Christmas card photo, and this photo, year after year, reveals nothing about us. We are styled, we match, no one's unique. My mom and I have the same hairstyles, soft, dark blond waves, having both been blown out and hot-rolled by Kat Pearson, my mom's stylist. My dad and Jay are matching, too: brown hair parted to the side, chests puffed out, jaws clenched, laughing through their teeth until it's over.

In last year's card you can't tell my mom is pregnant. She wanted to hide it for as long as possible, afraid she'd miscarry. In another, a couple of years before that, you can't see Jay's hangover or how sad we all are that my grandmother just died. You can never see how stressed I am from school and skating. All you can see is a girl who is confident, perhaps aloof, with a happy family, a beautiful home, a perfect, enviable life.

I walk down the hall, as if at a museum, and stop before this year's Christmas photo. The dress code: jeans and white sweaters, good god. Sammy's first card—he's ten months old. My dad looks like a king. Even the signs of aging—the little pouches under his eyes, the forehead fissures—give him strength. You would never know from this year's photo that he's been wrongly accused of robbing people blind or that he'll spend our winter break in a courtroom.

My brother walks out of his room. He looks like he's just woken up.

"Jay!" I hear my mom call from downstairs. "Annie!"

"You always get called first," I say.

"Because I'm older, and I'm meant to herd you."

We walk down the staircase. Our parents sit in the living room in front of the fireplace. The wall of glass behind them makes it seem like the snow and forest are part of our space. My mom sits on the black leather chair next to the plush sectional. She looks so formal, like she's about to give a presentation. My baby brother is in his ExerSaucer gnawing on his knuckle. I'm so glad he's here, that he exists—one, because I love his fat face, and, two, so my mom can stop trying to have a baby. The fertility drugs made her wicked.

"Have a seat," my dad says, gesturing to the couch. His face is pinched and cold. He usually looks like he's waiting for the punch line of a joke even when he's being serious. The sides of his hair are streaked with gray—they make me think of a road, which makes me think of riding with him on his motorcycle, my hands around his waist, holding on for dear life on the curves. I'd rest my cheek on his leather jacket. My mom would get nervous, but not that much when I think about it. I don't know if she trusted him completely or didn't have a choice, or didn't want one. My mom takes care of their social lives.

Jay and I sit on opposite sides of the couch. I try my best to look composed.

Jay claps his hands together. "What's up?"

I scoff. His attitude is so kiss-ass positive. Always so relaxed. It's a man thing and I am a girl. I just hold on for dear life. Except I don't. I know my dad. I know real estate. The difference is Jay and I can have the same things in life, but he won't have to study.

My mom dabs at her shirt: boob-milk leakage.

"As you know, Dad will be in Denver for a while," my mom says. "The attorneys think it's best that I'm also at court. To show support. So we'll both be going. We'll stay at the Cheesman Park apartment."

"Would it help if we were there, too?" I ask, and get a nasty look from Jay.

"No, sweetie," my dad says. "It'll be boring. You guys have a good break."

My parents then stop and look at one another.

"You're going to stay with Aunt Nicole and Uncle Skip while we're away," my mom says.

"What?" I ask. "Why?"

"That's cool," Jay says, most likely thrilled, since they live in Breckenridge and he can snowboard every day.

"Why can't Jay and I stay here by ourselves? I can handle things just fine." *Better than you,* I think.

"I'm sorry," she says. "These are hard times, but we'll make the best of it. This is all we can do."

Really? I think. *This is all we can do?*

"Or, we can all just live together," I say.

"It's temporary," my dad says. "The trial shouldn't go on for long. A few weeks. If it's longer, you may have to commute to school for a bit—"

"Commute? Why would we do that from Breckenridge and not Denver with you?"

"It's going to be stressful," he says, ignoring me. "Every day I'll be prepping with lawyers. It's best if you guys aren't around all that."

"It's better . . . you're away." My mom gives us a brief, shaky smile, and I feel for her just then. She's a fifty-year-old woman in teenager-like clothes. She's had a face-lift and a boob "refill." She has never had to work, and now this.

"What's happening?" I ask. "You made it sound like this wouldn't be a big deal. Everyone at school was staring at me, Mackenzie Miller made it seem like . . . like you're some kind of criminal, and Cee won't return my texts."

My parents look at one another again.

"Her dad is testifying, that's all," my dad says. "She's probably just concerned."

"Testifying how?" I ask.

"Against us," my mom says, and her words ring in my head and stay there: *against us.* Against us. We're not on the same side, after all.

"Look," my dad says, and leans forward, as if we're all in on something together. "The attorneys are confident, but the DA needs to make a statement and it could get uncomfortable. I can take it, but you guys shouldn't have to, okay? Skip and Nicole are really looking forward to having you."

Nicole is my mom's younger sister, and all I know is they have some kind of ongoing feud, which is why this is so confusing.

"We don't even know them," I say. "Why can't we stay with friends?"

"You don't have any," Jay says.

I'm about to throw a dig back, but his statement settles within me, finding its home. *Cee is my friend,* I want to say, but this sounds babyish, and right now it doesn't seem like an option anyway.

"We should get a ruling by the end of your break. Perfect timing, and we'll take it from there," my mom says. She looks lost, as if she's delivering a memorized speech that sounded good in her head but isn't working out loud. She looks back at Sammy, then to us. "I want you to be able to have fun," she says. "That may mean . . . you know, leaving here, and maybe . . . not telling anyone who you are."

I'm hoping my dad will be mirroring my disbelief and disgust, but he's not. He's looking down at the floor.

"Nicole and Skip are going to say that you're their niece and nephew, but from Skip's side of the family—just in case anyone makes the connection or knows . . . the history."

"Are you serious? That's ridiculous." I stand up and look down at her. "Why would we do that?"

"You're Skip's brother's kids coming for a visit. You're the Towns," my dad says.

Jay laughs. "It's not like we're felons or something."

"Just, please," my mom yells, and Jay and I quickly lose our grins. "This is big news. There are a lot of angry people out there, and I want you to be safe."

"Safe?" I ask.

"Not safe, but . . . I don't want anyone judging you." She looks down. "Alienating you. You just said everyone at school was staring."

I roll my eyes, but it's then that I know these things are happening to her. That's why we're all getting out. They're trying to protect us by sending us to some dirty ski town.

She wrings her hands, then stands up, looking impatient and preoccupied. Her hair is blown out, and when she moves, it doesn't move with her. We have the same kind of round face, almond eyes, and thin, odd nose, rounded at the bottom in a heart shape. Our hair is the same—brown-blond and thick, but hers is dyed a brighter shade.

She walks to me, grabs my hand. It feels bony yet soft. She smiles, briefly, when I squeeze back. This is as affectionate as she gets.

"You won't want to be around us," my mom says. "Trust me. And you don't want to stay here."

"But when we win, we can come back," I say, and look at my dad.

"Of course—" he says, but my mom cuts in, which surprises me.

"If he wins, the people who lost their money don't win." Her brow is furrowed, and she worries the cuff of her sleeve. For the first time, I'm wondering if she believes in my father. He's not looking at her, and I know they've been fighting.

She gets Sammy, then walks to the stairs, touching Jay's shoulder on the way.

"Why don't you guys pack up," my dad says.

"Now?" I ask.

"You'll leave on Sunday, the day after Christmas."

"That's in two days!" I say. "That's the entire break."

Jay gets up and goes. We've just been told we're moving to

a stranger's house and that we should hide our identities, and he just gets up and goes. Our whole lives we've been told to represent our family name, to live up to it, and now we're told to deny it, to pretend we're someone else. Yet, I guess I understand the logic of getting out until things blow over. While I don't want to live with my aunt and uncle, I don't want to face anyone, either. Being at Evergreen assured me of that.

"What's Ken going to say when he testifies?" I ask. Ken is Cee's father and someone I'm close to. I have spent so much time at their house, watching movies, playing chess, cooking, hiking—I can't imagine being on a different side as them. I can't imagine him betraying us this way.

Dad looks up, his face tense with anger. "Don't worry about Ken."

"I *am* worried!" I say. "You said these things happen in real estate, but—"

"Yes, these things happen," he says, his voice scaring me. "It's not like I hold people at gunpoint, demanding their money." He stands up. "It's complex. And I don't need you accusing me—"

"I wasn't accusing you!" My voice breaks. "I'm trying to understand."

He actually walks out. He's annoyed with me, angry with me, his complacent, perfect girl. He doesn't think I'm capable of understanding, which I know I am. I cry, but put a hand over my mouth. I don't know what I'm crying about. I just feel abandoned and ashamed. I feel like my life just changed in an instant.

I walk past the living room table with the bowl of Christmas cards we've gotten this year. Some family I don't know is on top, posed by a lake. One kid is lying on his back, propped up on his elbows, making a silly face, his eyes crossed. The other kid is running out of the water. The parents are smiling, but the mom is looking at some other camera. You can tell it's the kind of picture that only at a later date was designated to be The Card. This is the kind of photo I like. The moment is caught. The people are revealed. They weren't thinking of an audience. They were just being themselves.

3

My parents and Sammy have left for Denver. Usually I feel free when both parents are gone, but instead I'm unsure of every step. I walk down the hall to my brother's room to rally him into being negative with me.

"Knock, knock," I say when I reach his open door.

He looks up from his guitar, fingers still poised to pluck. Jay is a senior. He puts little effort into getting people to like him, and yet everyone does.

His girlfriend, Sadie, is on his bed, lying down all casually, but she's totally trying to be sexy, and it looks false, like a model in a magazine striking an unlikely pose on a park bench. She looks like she's about to crawl through a low tunnel. Loose curls and dark full eyebrows hold her face in place. Her anime-like eyes are set above high cheekbones. I can't imagine being so relaxed, so overtly sexual. My freshman year, I went out with a junior—a lacrosse player who ended up cheating on me with someone from his class. A girl like Sadie, whose every move is designed for others to see. I wouldn't have sex with him. So he found someone who would.

"Are you packed?" I ask Jay.

"Yup," he says.

He strums on his guitar. His clothes are draped over his desk chair, still on their hangers.

"I can't believe you're leaving," Sadie says. When she talks, it sounds like she's gagging on her words.

"It'll be *fine*," Jay says, as if egging on a friend to jump off a bridge with him.

"So you're happy with this situation?" I lean against his door.

"Of course I'm not happy," he says.

"I'm the opposite of happy," Sadie says.

"So you guys are the same," I say, and Sadie seems to be figuring out some complicated math.

"I don't see why you can't live with me," she says.

Jay shrugs. I have a feeling he isn't terribly put out, that he can cope just fine with a little distance from her. As with every girl he's been with, she's like Velcro.

I look out his window to the same view I have of the backyard, guesthouse, pool, and aspen forest. I wonder what our new view will be like. What's happening to us? Jay looks up from the guitar and sings while making eye contact. I can tell he's feeling the same way—worried about the future—but we're both tamping things down, either trying to protect or outlast one another.

"What if your dad doesn't, like, win?" Sadie asks. She looks around the room as if afraid to lose something that isn't even hers. "Could he go to jail? I mean, serial killers are in jail." Her butt tilts up, punctuating her fear.

"Really, Sadie?" I say. "They put serial killers in jail? No way!"

"Hon, it's not that kind of jail," Jay says to her. "Remember Martha Stewart? When she went to prison, she taught yoga and made a nativity scene out of ceramics. Plus, my dad doesn't lose."

"And he didn't do anything wrong," I say. And Jay's right. Dad doesn't lose and he never settles, which makes me think of Cee and her dad. What are they thinking? What happened?

I text her again:

I know your dad's testifying. Why? Talk!

"Are you almost ready?" I ask.

"Yup," he says.

"I'll be downstairs." I head down, looking at my phone, the dots telling me she's typing, erasing, typing. Finally, a message:

We R done.

I sit on the piano bench and wait, shaking my knee up and down, lightly tapping my fist on the keys. I'm packed and ready to go, and am impatient now to reach a destination I don't want to get to in the first place. What does she mean, *we're done*? It pisses me off—how can she dismiss our friendship with one text? *I* didn't do anything. Our dads may not be getting along, but that doesn't mean you flee. I slam the piano keys. The house is too quiet. Outside, the snow is shaded with a gray light—it's like we're orphans in a dystopian land, and any moment I'll have to run for cover or be assigned to some kind of faction. I bang middle C.

Jay comes down the stairs holding his clothes, all still on their hangers. His guitar is strapped to his chest, his backpack on his back. If we were in a dystopian thriller, Jay would survive just because others would want him around. Sadie trails behind him, her hand on his shoulder to balance herself on her high-heeled sneakers. She'd die in the first scene and no one would cry.

"Ready?" Jay asks.

"Been ready," I say. "My stuff's in the car."

"You eager or something?"

"No, just efficient." C sharp, C minor.

By his look, I can tell he's displeased. Maybe by having me as a sister, his companion for this strange trip. Or maybe he sees that I'm a bit lost, that he's in charge now, and he isn't prepared.

Outside, I wait some more. I wait in the car while he puts our snowboards on the roof. I wait while he loads the trunk. I wait while he says good-bye to Sadie. I'm in the front seat. They're on the other side toward the back. I stare straight ahead at our house; perched on a rock wall, it glows from the inside. Through all the tall glass windows—the fireplace, the stairs, and the piano. I know we'll be back soon, but I'm the kind of person who always wants to go home, and now I won't be able to.

"Seriously wish your sister wasn't here right now," I hear Sadie say. And then in a singsong voice: "I'd go down on you."

Oh my god, I'm internally hurling. I don't hear anything, which means they're kissing. I'm repulsed, though at the same time, I wish I had someone to miss, someone to kiss, someone who'd be closing their eyes, too. Even a friend to see me off would be nice. I keep thinking that Cee will show, but I give up. She's not coming.

Finally, Sadie walks in front of the windshield and throws me a bitchy wave. I give her a thumbs-up, as in, good job skedaddling. Good job being a girl who'd give a farewell bj. Peace.

But then I feel bad because after she gets in her SUV, she wipes her face below her eyes. My brother gets in, and I wonder if he wants to cry too. I doubt it, but still I make myself stay quiet, because even when I try to say something nice, a little bitterness jumps out like a flea.

He reverses out of the driveway, then drives ahead slowly. We both look left at our house, the beautiful mass of it, like a castle in the sky. It's early evening now, and our neighbors' homes are lit up with Christmas lights. Ours are out.

"This is so weird," I say.

"We're not going very far," Jay says.

4

We haven't gone far, yet we have gone oh so far. When we enter the town of Breckenridge, I get nervous, like it's my first day at school or a new sport. We've never skied here, which is strange, considering we have family here, but we always go past it to Vail or Aspen.

"This is kind of ghetto," I say. We drive by a set of dark brown condos that look like a motel.

He pats my shoulder, kind of hard. "There, there," he says.

"There, there?"

"There, there—man up. How's that?"

We drive slowly down the main road, which looks about a block long. Jay puts some song on the stereo and it makes this seem even more eventful than it should be. I swear, he makes me feel bad through music.

"Look," he says. "Steak and Rib."

I look to the left and there it is—my uncle's restaurant, STEAK AND RIB, which is in need of a paint job. A parrot is painted on the sign, a touch of real snow on the wooden feathers. Seriously. Why a parrot? Just. Why?

"We can probably eat there all the time," Jay says.

"Oh, great," I say, looking away. "Free steak. And rib."

At what looks to be the end of town, he turns off the main road, then into a residential neighborhood. It's a nice, comfy-looking street with big new homes and pretty Christmas lights, a little reminiscent of our neighborhood in the winter. I sit up a bit.

"I missed the turn," Jay says, checking the GPS, and my anticipation is shot. We're not on the right street, and I bet nothing around here is any better.

"I can't believe we've never even been to their house," I say.

Jay drives back down to Main Street, then into a different neighborhood.

"This is crazy," I say. "Our backwoods relations. They probably have skinny dogs. Did Dad fuck up or what." I drop my words off, all nonchalant.

"No," Jay says after a while. "Other people got in over their heads. Now he has to deal with it. It'll work out."

"It better," I say.

We drive past Steak and Rib again, then Jay turns into a different area, the homes smaller and older. They all look the same.

"Look for 431," he says.

I look out my window. "On your left, dummy."

He slows down in front of a house with curtains that look like doilies, then another with curtains that look like a grannie's apron. He goes forward, stops again in front of a small green house.

"This is it," he says.

White curtains, basic and drawn, so hopefully they don't know we're here yet.

"Let's scope things out," I say, though there isn't a lot to scope. The house is basically the size of our garage.

In front of their neighbor's house is an inflated Santa riding a motorcycle along with lit-up, mechanized lawn angels. The Santa is making a racket, like a blender set on Stir.

"It seems like the poorer you are, the more Christmas shit you have," I say.

"That's a snobby thing to say," Jay says.

"It does sound snobby," I say. "But I think it's a pretty accurate observation."

He shrugs. He's happy because he's unobservant, and I didn't mean to sound snobby. I kind of like the lawn decorations. We were never able to decorate our tree or string lights because someone is always hired to do that. My friends' homes always had such odd things—fake mini trees in a Santa boot, ornaments with their faces on them, a collection of nutcrackers, some things beautiful, some things hideous, but all of them fun or holding meaning and memory. Secretly, I have always wanted Christmas shit, even though I roll my eyes alongside my mom when she declares things cheesy.

"Home, sweet home," Jay says.

"Not home, not sweet," I say.

"Should we go knock?" He opens his door.

"You knock, Jay Town." I laugh, but then realize it sounds kind of cool: J-Town. And I am A-Town. Not bad.

He gets out, and I follow, feeling like an urchin or a foster child. I take a bag so I have something to hold, something to do with my hands.

We walk up the path to the front door. I can hear a television and smell something cooking, something fishy yet tough and steaklike. Shrimp, I bet. Barbecue.

Jay knocks on the door. I clear my throat, and Jay seems to relax his shoulders, and then my uncle Skip opens the door, his face full of happiness and light, his brown eyes moving all over us. I can't help but smile. He looks like he's welcoming the hosts of a surprise home-makeover show.

"Hey, guys!" he says. "Look at you." He hesitates, not knowing if he should hug us or shake our hands, but then he hugs me, somewhat roughly, patting my back on the way out of the hug. I've noticed after puberty, you get hugged differently.

"Annie!" he says.

"Hello," I say, warmed by something in his face—a confusion similar to my own, and yet a casualness and gameness that makes me feel safe. He almost looks like a college student—the kind who doesn't graduate on time. Skip Town—ha! I only just put this together now, which really proves how little they're in our lives.

He hugs Jay heartily, takes him in, hits his back, ruffles his hair.

"Uncle Skip," Jay says, and hits his shoulder. Why do guys always have to hit their hellos? "Looking good."

"Come on in," Skip says. "God, it's been years! You're human-sized!"

I feel like I'm meeting future Jay. Another person who only thinks about one thing at a time. We walk in, but I stay close to the door.

"We're here," I say, for some reason.

"You're here!" Skip says. "Do you have more stuff?" He hits himself on his forehead with the palm of his hand. "Of course you do."

"Finally!" My aunt Nicole comes from the hall in a way that seems calculated, like she was waiting in the wings for her cue. I haven't seen her in so long, and yet she kind of looks the same. Like someone still growing.

"We were wondering when you'd show up." She walks closer, then greets me with a stiff embrace. She's a distant hugger, taking my shoulders and sort of shaking them. She's so different from my mom—she's sporty and unfiltered, doesn't put as much thought into her appearance. She and Skip both look so at a loss that it's almost endearing. It's like they've never dealt with kids before and wish they had a manual.

Someone sighs.

"You guys must be tired," Skip says, as if we've come from Uzbekistan.

"Super tired," I say, and yawn, and still I'm standing by this damn door.

Nicole picks up a glass of wine from a table by the couch and takes a big sip.

"*The Price Is Right to Remain Silent*," she says, and Jay and I give each other looks, sharing the awkwardness. We both half laugh, but then she gestures to the TV, which is on *Wheel of Fortune*. Some lady in a pantsuit solves the puzzle moments after Nicole. Now she's clapping and bouncing and saying, "Woo!"

I smile at Nicole, congratulating her, but she appears to give zero fucks about her puzzle-solving skills.

"We have more stuff outside," Jay says.

"I'll help you out with that," Skip says. "Or are you guys hungry? I made this Thai beer shrimp—"

"I knew it!" I say, which makes everyone look at me like I'm a freak instead of a person who likes to cook.

"Beer shrimp," Jay says. "Wow."

"Yeah, it's not alcoholic or anything—we wouldn't serve alcohol. It's just in the marinade." Skip pantomimes whisking a sauce.

"Beautiful," I mumble, and I mumble because my sincere comments are often taken as sarcasm or, as Jay would say, "snobbiness." But no. By "beautiful," I mean beautiful. The lemongrassy tang of Thai. The buttery malt of beer. I would never have thought of that.

"Great," Jay says, his hands on his hips, head pecking. "The kitchen, wow. Nice."

"You should have seen it before," Nicole says. "It looked like . . . the rest of the house."

Jay and I assess the rest of the house. It's very dark—dark walls, an itchy-looking couch, and like, no space, no amenities. Jay eyes me, urging me to say something. I look around, trying my best.

"Cool stools," I say, and we all look at the bar stools, which aren't that cool at all.

"It's been so long since we've seen you guys," Nicole says, something catching in her voice.

We're all so nervous it's unbearable. I feel like doing a jig just to get it all out. *Let's jig!* I want to yell.

"Super long," Jay says.

"How are your parents?" she asks, then shakes her head. "Stupid question."

Skip looks down with a furrowed brow as if he's figuring out a problem. He takes in a sip of air. "You guys must be going through a lot."

"We're fine," Jay says.

"We're fantastic," I say, and Nicole cringes and looks to her husband, for guidance it seems.

"Well, we're here for you," he says. "Whatever you need."

Nicole claps her hands together. "Let's bring your things to your rooms, then get the rest of your stuff."

This order brings relief to all of us.

Nicole leads us to our bedrooms, and I'm hit by a wave of homesickness, a longing for my parents I haven't had since my first year of summer camp six years ago, when I was ten. My mom had given me Atkins bars to keep me fit for ice-skating, but our counselor threw them out and told me, "Camp is your chance to change your destiny."

Since I'm supposed to be hiding, maybe it's time to change my destiny again, though I'm not sure what that would mean or what I'd be giving up.

We walk down a short hallway with wood walls that have lots of framed pictures. Not like our pictures with identical frames, but a patchwork of colorful photos. All hang a bit crookedly. I look, not wanting to really look, not wanting to see myself and Jay on the wall, or maybe not wanting to see our absence. I'd be embarrassed that Nicole would be embarrassed if I noticed either scenario. I'm always embarrassed for other people's embarrassment. It's embarrassing.

Nicole sees me lost in the wall, and she straightens one of the frames, then opens a bedroom door.

"This can be yours," Nicole says to Jay.

I take a quick glance into the room—it's bleak and small. I mean, it's fine. I've been in rooms like these, in houses like these. When I was younger, I had friends whose parents worked for Coors. It's funny because their homes were smaller, but they had tons more toys. My mom never let us have plastic toys that "marred" her landscape.

"Awesome," Jay says, and walks in.

Nicole walks a few steps to the next room, which is just as minimalistic. "And this one yours," she says. "Or whatever. You can switch."

I walk into mine. Then I walk right back out to fully compare.

His is smaller, I think. The bed has a purple comforter and lots of purposeless pillows that don't match one another. There's a sad, bulky TV that looks like it's from the '90s and a window that looks out to a brown backyard, telephone poles, and another identical house. God, I miss our house.

"Great," my brother says, and pushes on the bed like a mattress salesman. Nicole looks around as if it's the first time she's been in here.

"I know you're probably used to better things," she says.

"Not at all," he says, and I roll my eyes. She sees this, and I smile to cover it up.

"Sorry," I automatically say.

"No, it's okay," Nicole says. "I said it, and you . . . followed through."

"I didn't mean—"

"Don't worry about it," she says.

I walk to the other room, and though it's a tad larger than Jay's, it's pretty sad. It's clearly a kind of storage closet. There's an old TV, shelves of knickknacks, vases, movies on tape: *Out of Africa* and *Pretty Woman*, which I saw once on VH1. Loved it.

Skip walks in delicately as if he doesn't want to catch something.

"This okay?" he says.

I look down. "Yeah." It's much harder to be rude to him. His eyes always have that half-full look.

"There's a lot of stuff in here," he says. "Hey, Nicole?" he calls to the other room. "Maybe we could clear some of the stuff off the shelves?"

The shelves line an entire wall. They're filled with books and jewelry boxes and clay bowls that look like Mother's Day gifts.

"It's okay," I say, wanting to seem like I'm a girl who can camp and skip showers. "I'll manage." I think of the frontierswoman Calamity Jane, how she endured and conquered. Though she did have bad skin, a life of drudgery, and she drank like a salmon going upriver.

Nicole comes in and again looks around like it's her first time in here since they moved in.

"Sorry," she says. "This all happened so quickly." She walks toward the shelves. "Take down whatever. Just be careful—" She looks at Skip. "Or don't," she says. "Throw it out the window." She laughs a little, then sighs, I think as a way to pass the time. I smile politely and start to take things out of my suitcase to show my gameness. Unfortunately, one of my cowboy hats— the felt Billy Jack—is on top, slightly crushed. The Towns eye one another when I place it on the bed.

"Nice," Skip says, touching the beaded band.

"I collect them," I say.

"Wow," she says. "Cowboy hats?"

"From different Westerns. This one—" I pick it up, flip it onto my head. "Tom Laughlin's from *Billy Jack*. Not the actual one, but . . ."

They're both looking at me like I'm not quite real. Like they think I've been replaced by a different girl. I don't tell them Poz and Mira, our live-in help, gave me my first hat, that the most memorable parts of my childhood were watching Westerns with them, something we still do. I wonder how much Poz and Mira know. They always go to Arizona in December to visit their sons. They must have been warned that things might be different when they return.

"I know we're only here for a week or so," I say. "But I like having them around."

"Nothing wrong with that," Skip says. "Like a lovie."

"I didn't say there was anything wrong with it," Nicole says. "Anyway. I have pie."

I don't stop unpacking, not knowing how to respond. She has her hands on her hips and looks like I should be writing something down.

"I have pie!" she says again toward the hallway, louder so Jay can hear. She shrugs, then walks toward the door. "When you guys get settled, come out. We'll have dinner and some pie?"

"Okay! Thanks," I hear Jay say. I hear him *exclaim!!* How I despise exclamation-pointed words.

I dig back into my suitcase to hide my eyes, and when they

leave, I put on my steel-gray Virgil Earp with the turndown brim. There's a mirror over the desk. I look at myself, channeling the outlaw Josey Wales.

"Get ready, little lady. Hell is coming to breakfast."

When I've done all I want to do in my new room, I look out into the hall, then run over to Jay's. His door is partially closed. I kick it open a little. He's lying on the bed and talking on his phone. I walk around his new digs. The vinyl blinds are open. In the neighbor's yard a wolflike dog is moving a tin bowl around with his nose. Maybe it's not a wolflike dog. Maybe it's a wolf.

I stand in front of his bed and do this thing that I like to do— sort of like a trust fall, but you fall forward with your arms by your side, then once you hit the mattress you swoop your legs up so you look like a banana. Jay smiles at me while he talks to whomever. This move has cracked him up since we were little. I bounce on the bed and look at a globe on the desk, wondering what other sixteen-year-olds are doing right now. Sleeping, eating, kissing, driving. I'm most envious of the ones who are doing something super mundane and having a blast.

Who's having the most fun? Who's having the least? Someone could be getting killed. This thought makes me feel so small. I always think about that after I hear about a plane crash. Everyone just down here at their office or at school or Snapchatting in the car. Meanwhile people are up in the sky, praying for their lives, screaming, weeping, too much in the moment of terror to even think of envying us. It's goddamn horrible.

"It is," Jay says on the phone. "Yup. Miss you. I'm about to eat some pie. No! Like pie pie, silly. Cherry or pumpkin. I know. It all sounds sexual . . . Ha! Or pudding. Rhubarb."

Gross. I stand and go back to my den of sorrows to wait for him there. I'm met with a musty scent, a muggy weather. I walk to the shelf and check out the trinkets. A plush yellow duck, little bowls, and notecards, ceramics and vases, like the adult equivalent of shit you get in goodie bags. I swipe things to the side, spilling a few objects, then begin to put my hats up. I wonder what Sammy is doing now. Eating yogurt? Pulling himself to standing? Then I remember that he's probably asleep, the happiest baby in the world.

"Nice room," Jay says.

"The drawers are full of sweaters. It's like a refugee camp."

He puts his hands on his hips and nods. "Yeah, I'm sure this is really similar to a refugee camp. Jesus, you're seriously so spoiled."

He walks over to my bed, the heaps of clothes still on top.

"Like you're not?" I ask. I know I'm spoiled. It's not that I think it's so bad. It's that it's not home. I'm mad at our parents.

"You brought your own comforter." He pinches it between his fingers.

"Of course I did."

"I mean, who brings their own linens and shit when they visit someone?" He looks out my window, and I wonder if he's thinking about our old view, the lovely aspens slicing up the light.

"Mom told me to. She said I'd definitely prefer my own."

We look at each other, realizing this is kind of lame of her, and yet he eyes my pillows from home, maybe wishing he'd thought of doing the same. He looks around. "New digs. An adventure, right?" He's trying his best to be positive, but I catch a look of total disappointment. He's always had the attitude that there's no use complaining about something you can't fix. I've always had the attitude to complain as much as possible and try to get others to do so with you because it's more fun that way.

"What are you going to do?" I whisper.

He knows what I'm talking about. He looks toward the door, then shrugs.

"Should we go out there?" he whispers back.

"I guess so," I say.

"He has beer shrimp!" he whispers. "And she has pie!"

"Beer shrimp and pie!" I loud-whisper back.

The shrimp was so good. And the pie is, too. We sit at the dining room table. *Dancing with the Stars* is on the television behind us, but I can't tell who the stars are.

"So, Annie," Skip says, "you like cowboys and such?"

"What?" I say, my mouth full of chocolate.

"Cowboys," he says, his chin tilted up to keep the food in.

"I like Westerns," I say. "And fashion. I don't, like, play cowboys or, like, hang out with ranchers. Poz and Mira—they help out around the house—they got me into the films, and . . . I don't know. Some people collect baseball cards, I collect hats. Not too deep. We don't need to analyze it."

"I think Uncle Skip here is trying to make conversation," Jay says, and I wipe some cream off my nose with my middle finger.

"Yeah, I like cowboys and such," I say.

Skip laughs, which throws me off a bit. Perhaps he gets my humor and lack thereof.

"Annie's not quite socialized," Jay says, and winks at me.

Seriously, though. Some kids skateboard; some kids watch Westerns. I don't know why. Maybe it's just what I took on, like an accessory. Like skating, but something unique I chose for myself. I like the wildness of Westerns, the lawlessness, which ends up revealing the goodness in people, the strength. I like the view back into beginnings.

"Your mom says you do well in school, though?" Nicole says.

Though, as in at least I have that.

"And skating, of course," she adds.

I grip my spoon like it's a Ping-Pong paddle. Skip and Jay are chewing and waiting for me to respond. Why is everyone focused on me? It's like I just got out of rehab or something.

"Yes," I say, in a totally socialized way. "Of course."

"But that ship has sailed," Jay says. "Her coach gave up on her."

"Motherfucker," I say.

"Wow!" Nicole says.

"I told you!" Jay says. "She's not quite mature yet. Still teething. Don't be fooled by her posh exterior."

Skip clears his throat. I cut my crust, annoyed I'm always candid with my brother—I belly flop on his bed, I tell him about feeling rejected by Coach—and he uses it against me.

"I was getting tired of it anyway." This is only partially true. I was tired of it in the way I've always been tired of it. Because it was exhausting. Because it was my life. But I wasn't prepared

32

for my coach to say he needed to focus on the girls who were headed to Sun Valley for the summer competition, something I had thought I'd be doing myself. I told my mom I could just continue with someone else. I didn't need the best. I didn't need to be trained to be the best anymore. I could just skate. For fun.

"You don't *just* skate for fun," my mom said, then held up her hand, her sign for *I can't deal with you right now.*

Sixteen years old and fired from a sport, and yet I wonder if she took it harder. It was her sport, really. What she did when she was younger. Every sport I wanted to try when I was younger—soccer, volleyball, snowboarding—immediately shut down. Fierce athleticism is acceptable only in sequins and short skirts.

I think about the way I've been judged since I was a child. Were they looking at my Biellmann spin or my Vera Wang skating dress or, perhaps, my glorious crotch shot to the tune of Beyoncé's "Halo"? Yes, you *can* see my halo. I shake myself out of this horrid memory, which makes me smell the ice, feel the sensation of being locked in a freezer.

I notice everyone looking at me, so I dig into the pie with gusto. Dessert is something I'd typically go easy on, but hey, I'm fired. I'm free. I'm devastated, though it wasn't until I stopped skating that I realized it's the identity I miss, not so much the act of it.

"So, Jay," Skip says, "your dad tells me you're a big snowboarder. So is Nicole."

"Is that right?" Jay asks with a winning smile. He is really bringing out the violence in me.

"I'm okay," Nicole says. "Everyone's okay."

"She's good in powder and trees," Skip says. "That's a sign of being truly good."

"It's true," Jay says.

"What Skip means is that I can keep up with him," she says. "That makes me awesome. That I can keep up with an average male."

I smile a bit but try to hide it, letting my laugh escape through my nostrils. I'm charged by her negativity, and it occurs to me that Nicole's social skills might be right on par with mine. Maybe that's why my mom is always saying her sister needs to do better with her life. I imagine Nicole trying to talk to my mom's friends, how they'd widen their eyes and make excuses to refill their Chardonnays. Maybe she's not the worst.

"Annie, do you ride?" Skip asks. "Or ski? Maybe we all should go—"

"I can," I say. "But I don't."

The truth is I love to ride. I go with Jay a lot, put my headphones on and charge all day, run after run. My mom doesn't know—thinks it's not a girl sport, and she didn't want me to get hurt for skating, but I would sneak off, put on my baggy black snow pants—the opposite of my leotard and tights.

"She's really good," Jay says, and I give him a shy look.

Firewood crackles and snaps, and I glance at the alluring flames. We have one of those fireplaces that work at the touch of a button, but I've always wanted one like this to be in solidarity with our ancestors. Though they'd probably want the electric one. Nostalgia can be stupid, I guess.

"I like your fireplace," I say. "Cozy."

They look at me like I'm a gorilla who did something human-like.

"Maybe you guys can help me chop wood one day," Skip says.

Jay and I both let out a staccato snort-laugh. There are certain words you just can't say around us, "wood" being one of them. Skip and Nicole look puzzled.

"So, I guess your parents want you to be Towns," Skip says, looking shy and a little pleased. "I mean, I don't think it's really going to come up or anything." He looks over at Nicole and seems a little sad. "Just if anyone asks—"

"You don't come from me," she says, still looking at Skip.

"From your side of the family," he says to her.

"Ridiculous," she mumbles.

"Well?" he says. "They just want you to have a clean slate while you're here, I guess. Get away from your last name. Not that there's anything wrong with it. It's a great last name, and you should be proud." He notices we're all staring at him, amused. "Anyway. It's so you can enjoy your vacation. Without judgment."

"Yes, your mom is very concerned about judgment."

"Hon, there's also the Desjarlais and—"

"Yeah, yeah, yeah," she says.

Jay and I look at one another, not understanding what the hell *Desjarlais* is all about, but understanding they're having some sort of hidden argument loaded with insider info.

"This is really good pie," Jay says to Nicole.

"I didn't make it," she says, looking at her empty plate with longing.

"What kind of pie is it?" he says.

"Turtle nut," she says.

"What?" he asks, his voice breaking a bit, and I hold back laughter.

"Turtle nut."

Jay and I both crack up, and Nicole and Skip exchange glances that seem to say, *What the nut did we sign up for?*

In room. Alone. First night. Lying in bed, staring at the TV, staring at the ceiling.

I need to use the bathroom but don't want to go into the hall in case someone's out there. It's so weird not having my own bathroom. I've never not had that before. Around fourteen more nights of this to go? And what if it's longer? Commuting? Coming back from school to *this*? How will I tolerate that? What pleases me, or comforts me, is the fact that I know how restless Jay must be. He's never alone, and now he is. I bet he's pacing, talking on the phone, texting, flipping channels. Ah, there it is. I smell the weed, get up from bed, and see smoke billowing out his window. I open my window and can hear him on the phone talking to someone, wanting to know what's going on tonight.

I stand still, doing something he can't.

I lie back down on my bed and continue to watch some show about catching child predators. Holy shit. I realize I need to get up to change channels. I won't be able to stand this for even one more day, let alone fourteen. I stand up, press the button on the side of the TV. The screen has a three-second delay after my push, and I'm about to break ass, so I just settle on PBS and return to bed, mumbling the phrase "I'm speakin' to you, pig shit," like it's my calming mantra, which, I guess, it is.

I tune in, sleepy and thankful for this tiredness. I listen to the narrator on the television, letting his words sink in, my brain doing what it will with this new information.

. . . *A moving record of Colorado's transformation. Here everything seems somehow larger, grander than life. It's easy to understand why so many different people see their innermost lives as inextricably linked to the ground upon which they stand. The story of Colorado is a series of triumphs, a relentless epic in which greed and cruelty are often glossed over as enterprise and courage.*

This is good. My eyelids feel like they're carrying tiny weights. I'm comforted by the fireplace out in the living room, the thought of blue and orange embers losing light.

5

Morning. Our first real day living here. I'm in this sad room, in a big T-shirt and small underwear. Do I need to get fully dressed to go out there? Can I wear what I'm wearing? Of course not. Usually, at least on school days, Mira brings breakfast to my room on a tray—coffee, fruit, two eggs—but now my peaceful mornings in a shirt and underwear are gone. I pull on some jeans, even though I absolutely hate eating breakfast with pants on. I walk out and hear Skip and Nicole talking in the kitchen, so I stop at the end of the hall.

"Put clothes on!" I hear Nicole say. "We have the kids now."

I guess Skip has to say good-bye to peace and underwear too.

"All right, all right," he says, and then appears in front of me with jeans on, but shirtless. Jay comes out of the bathroom, shirtless and in boxers.

"Morning, everyone," Skip says.

"Hi," I bleat, sheeplike. I have an uncle with abs.

"Morning," Jay says, all at ease with himself and his surroundings. "Your toilet has such a strong flush!"

"Oh, thanks," Skip says. "Go on out, get some breakfast." Skip pats Jay on the back. I see them in a fantasy football league; it's looming there on the horizon.

I do a thumbs-up, then walk out to the kitchen, cursing my thumb for going up like that. I am not a thumbs-upper or a high-fiver.

Nicole stands in the kitchen chugging water out of a glass. She's in tight running pants and a tight black shirt. Her collarbone looks like a boomerang. A black headband holds her hair off her face, and after putting down her water, she swoops it up into a ponytail. She looks ready to run a something-K. Her body puts me in mind of beef jerky. It's like some of the skater girls, just a few who are all muscle, and yet what is she training for?

"Morning," I say. I can't imagine it ever becoming comfortable here.

"Morning," she says, looking down. I realize that she's just as shy and uncomfortable as I am.

Except for her brown-blond hair, she doesn't look like my mom at all. Maybe it's the wardrobe; maybe it's the lack of maintenance; maybe it's because she's younger. She's pretty, in an effortless, natural way. A hidden way. She could be on the cover of *Granola Magazine*, if that existed. Or *Outdoor Salad. The Hike Within*. My mom is a different kind of pretty. Head-turning. You see her right away. She looks like you're supposed to think she's hot. She looks rich. It's funny to think how their different looks must have determined what happened to them in life. Even though I look more like my mom—I'm supposed to, both she and my father would freak if I didn't put an effort into my looks—I'm determined not to be like my mom. I don't want to be a trophy wife. I want to be the person who wins the trophies: my dad. That's why I work for him in the summers, why I work my ass off in school, and why I try to not let the small dramas of high school affect me. My dad doesn't have many friends either. They're a distraction.

I walk into the kitchen, not really knowing what I'm allowed to do.

"Help yourself to whatever," Nicole says. "No maid here."

"I was going to make some eggs," I say. I like to cook, and hope I'll still be able to. "If there are any. Should we get our own groceries?"

"No," she says. "It's all taken care of. Here." She opens the fridge and hands me a carton of eggs. "I can't believe how expensive they are these days."

Is she just making conversation or reminding me about the cost of things?

"Let's see." She scurries around the kitchen. "Here's a bowl and skillet and—just help yourself. Feel free to rummage around. Open cupboards to your heart's content."

"Thanks." I roam for ingredients, finding a spice rack, though the spices look dense and old. I open the canister of oregano and take a whiff.

"You should buy small quantities of this," I say.

She's staring at me as though thoroughly confused. Jay's right. I really don't know how to talk to people. My tone is all wrong. I smile to make up for its deafness.

"Short shelf life, that's all. Ha. Try saying that three times." I do it. "Short shelf life, short shelf life, short shelf life. Guess it wasn't that hard."

She looks at the oregano in my hand, then at me. "Okay," she says. "Noted."

"I wasn't being critical—"

She holds her hands up. "No, no, you just . . . sounded like your mom for a sec. She . . . criticizes a lot. I'm not saying you were criticizing."

"I was just suggesting." I take another whiff.

"She does that too! She *suggests*. Sorry. I just got off the phone with her, and . . ." She pulls on her tight shirt at the chest as if she needs air.

"What did she say?" I ask.

"Not much. She was heading out . . . to court." She cringes, knowing how strange that sounds.

"Oh," I say.

"Sorry," she says. "I don't have a lot to tell you. She doesn't really give me all the details."

"It's fine," I say. "I know what's going on."

She smiles with her mouth closed.

Last Christmas my four-year-old cousin who lives in New York told me he stays up very late with huge bowls of candy with all his friends on the top bunk. I looked at him and smiled in the way Nicole is looking at me now, like his self-delusions were cute and that I had to build his self-esteem.

"Skip said the same thing about the oregano," she says. "He said I bought too much."

Great. It's like I was just declared the winner. "Would you like an omelet?" I ask.

"No, thanks. I just ate, but thank you."

"I can cook," I say. "Earn my keep."

She grabs her ankle behind her and raises it to her butt. "You don't need to earn your keep. We're happy to have you."

I can tell this was hard for her to say. I start to move around again, gathering milk and a bowl and a whisk. The kitchen is actually kind of nice. I like the small size. It's like putting on a puppet show. I chop some small bell peppers and grate sharp cheddar. It's very good cheese. Skip must have bought it. It might be nice living with someone who owns a restaurant.

"So is cooking one of your hobbies, then?" Nicole asks, switching legs.

"Yes," I say. "It's something I do with—" I stop myself, not wanting to tell her it's something I do with Mira, not just because it sounds spoiled, this fact we have a cook, but also because it sounds sad—my mom didn't teach me to cook. The help did. "Something I do," I say.

I heat the peppers, and when the pan sizzles, I pour in the milky whisked eggs, tapping in salt and a bit of nutmeg. "Is running one of your hobbies?" I put the heat on low.

"It relaxes me," she says, but seems unsure about this. "It's supposed to."

Jay and Skip walk out from the hall, Jay wearing just his snow pants with the suspenders hanging.

"Then you don't have to deal with the line at the gondola," Skip says to Jay, and then eyes my skillet. "Whoa. Look at that."

Skip comes into the kitchen to look at my breakfast in the making. Jay follows. He sees Nicole's box of cereal and puts his hand in it.

"Morning, Aunt Nicole," Jay says. Nicole backs up against the sink. The cramped space is getting to her. There's a commotion in her kitchen, and she's probably used to being here alone in a big tee and small undies.

"Morning," she says.

"I was just telling Jay to catch the shuttle right to Peak Eight, then go to the T-bar. It's supposed to be good up there. Any plans today?" Skip asks, looking at the skillet, then my face.

"Um," I say. "Not really."

Skip and Nicole communicate. He raises his eyebrows and twists his mouth. She closes her eyes for a second and exhales. This seems to solve something.

"I'm okay on my own, though," I say, looking back and forth between the two. "I don't, like, need to be babysat."

"We know," Skip says. "Just thinking of things you can do while you're here. Don't want you to get bored. Hon, maybe you could see if Jen's daughter—"

"Who's Jen?" Nicole asks, putting on tight green gloves.

"Jen," he says, and pantomimes someone with either big boobs or who carries large sacks of groceries.

"Jen from work?" She plugs earphones into her phone, then straps it to her arm. I feel like I'm watching an assassin getting dressed. "She's a weirdo."

"Well, maybe her daughter isn't," Skip says.

"Her daughter's the one I'm talking about," Nicole says.

"Oh," he says.

"Okay, yeah, I gotta go to work," she says. "I'll give you guys some room."

Skip looks at me and Jay, and pantomimes jogging. "She runs to work."

"Wow," I say.

Nicole pushes Skip a bit against the dishwasher. "Excuse me, if I could get by."

She totally could have gotten by, but I guess this is the way she's going about delivering some kind of point.

"Have a good day!" Skip calls.

She leaves, slamming the front door. Jay and I exchange glances. It's quiet now, except for the sounds of my cooking.

"She's on meds that make her a little moody," Skip says.

We don't say a word.

"But she's not on them right now, though, so . . . I guess that's not why she's moody, and, well, I didn't need to tell you any of that. About the meds." He nods as if deciding on something. "We'll all get used to each other."

I put the finished product on a plate and slide it toward Skip. "What are the meds for?" I ask.

"Thanks so much," he says, opening a drawer and taking out three forks. "Wow. Beautiful. The drugs, yeah, uh, they're for babies. For having babies. Fertility." He walks around to the stools and has a seat.

"Oh." I pour in more eggy mixture for Jay. "Congratulations."

"For what?" Skip says.

"Yeah, for what?" Jay says. He leans on the counter across from us.

"I don't know—trying? Doing it. The whole baby thing, not *it* . . ." Damn. I put some green pepper in my mouth to keep me quiet.

"They say children are the future," Jay says.

"Shut up," I say. The pepper didn't work.

"We're super excited," Skip says.

I finish Jay's stupid omelet, not giving it as much time as

Skip's. I slide it across the small island as violently as possible, and he catches it in a way that lends the whole thing grace.

Skip sits next to Jay on the other bar stool. "This is great," Skip says. "Crispy on the outside and creamy in the middle. This is just delightful."

I cook mine and eat standing up. I wonder what Sammy's doing right now. It's crazy that he may just be sitting in his playpen, laughing and flapping his arms. What if that was part of my daily routine? *I'm just going to flap my arms, maybe cry and poop.* How long will it last for him?

"Sammy does this thing right now," I say. "His kissy face. He puckers up like this and stares at you." I imitate Sammy, and so does Jay. We both look at Skip with our kissy faces, and he responds with a huge smile. HUGE. It doesn't seem to take much to make him very happy.

"Classic!" Skip hits his thigh and laughs a deep belly laugh. "That's great." His smile comes down. "Look, I'm sorry about all of this. I don't know if you want to talk about anything or . . . if you don't want to talk about it at all or . . . if something is on the news, should I let you watch it?"

"Have you seen something today?" I ask.

"Well, in the paper today, there was a bit about his secretary filing a lawsuit. I guess she invested about thirty grand. She has a sick kid and . . ." Skip looks down. "It's kind of horrible."

My chest tightens. I like Joanie Lee. When I was little, I'd go to her office to wait for my dad and she'd give me candy and her iPad. It's a horrible situation, but it's not really his fault she decided to invest. If anything, he was giving her an opportunity.

"That's awful," I say, wishing she hadn't taken such a risk.

Skip nods and takes a bite of his omelet, head down, serious, like my eggs are Communion. He glances behind him at the living room. "This must be really disappointing. I mean, your house is huge."

This makes me feel bad about my snobbery. I wonder if my parents could just give them some money, at least for some nicer furniture.

"No, we're sorry we're putting you out," Jay says.

"You're not putting us out at all," Skip says, and I can tell he means it and that we may be something fun for him—something new he can sink his teeth into, like a chew toy.

"It's silly that we live so close and never spend time with you guys," he says.

"Why is that?" Jay lifts his fork, stretching the cheese. "You're like these strangers who we know."

It's true. That's exactly who they are—and why is this? Why don't we know my mom's only sister? Why don't we do Christmases together? I wonder if I can figure it out while I'm here. I can't imagine growing up and never speaking to Jay.

"That's going to change now," Skip says. "I'm fired up that you're here, and flattered—we're both very honored that you chose us."

Jay and I exchange glances, but remain silent, not wanting to burst his bubble. He reminds me of our old dog Linus, welcoming us home, even if we were gone for just a moment—he'd give a high-pitched hum-cry, wagging his body and peeing a little.

"We can be practice kids," I say. "Dummies. But then you'll probably want to get your tubes tied. Or whatever they do."

My jokes just don't go over very well, but Skip laughs anyway.

"Nicole's happy you're here, too." He rubs his face in a way that makes me think that he once had a beard.

I'm afraid I'm not hiding my skepticism very well. Jay slides his plate toward me, and I catch it, then put it in the sink.

"It's going to work," Skip says. "I want you to feel at home here for the next week. Or two. However long."

I finish my bite. "Well, I never found home that great, but let's go."

Skip shakes his head, gives me a teasing smile like I'm just joking. I am, in a way—it's a line from *A Fistful of Dollars*—but when I delivered the quote, I felt like I was saying something a little true, because now that I'm not home, I'm not sure what it is that I miss.

6

It's nice with both Skip and Nicole gone. I can roam the house and open drawers and closet doors. I can use the bathroom in peace. I can scope out the food situation.

I read the titles of books on the shelf by the fireplace: *Winsor Pilates*, *Colorado Settlers and Native Americans*, *The Truth About Sporting Dogs*. So . . . what is the truth?

"Hey," Jay says, walking from the hall, now fully dressed for outdoor adventure. "I'm outs. Want to come with?"

"I don't know." I keep looking at books. He knows that *I don't know* means *no*.

I pull *What to Expect When You're Expecting* off the shelf. My mom should have lent Nicole all her books on pregnancy and infertility and child raising. Maybe that's why Nicole doesn't like my mom—she's jealous of her fertility, jealous of her wealth, her looks, her abundance.

I continue to scan the shelves for more info. In my mom's room, I once came across *The Explosive Child* and knew that the explosive child was me. When I was a toddler, I was oppositional and emotional, and my parents had to combat that with praise. I was like a shrew they had to tame. On her shelf I also saw *The Dangers of Helicopter Parenting*, which I didn't get at all. Not the subject matter, but why my mom would have a book like that in the first place. She's more of a satellite parent. Well, maybe not when it comes to skating and clothes and social expectations. In those areas I can hear the engine nearby.

I wonder what's happening in court right now. I imagine a lawyer giving an ovation-worthy speech, my dad and mom hugging. We could go back to school vindicated and victorious.

I open the *Expecting* book to a penciled fetus.

"What if we hear them?" I ask and hold up the book. "You know." I circle my hips and do a little move with my arms and point my fingers.

"What was that?" Jay imitates my sex move and laughs. "The Sprinkler? The *Scarface* hula? Say aloha to my little friend."

"Shut up," I say, totally embarrassed. I don't know sex moves. Jay's the slutface around here. I'm so worried that the first time I have sex the guy will do the same thing: say, *What was that?* and laugh. I don't want to have sex for a million years. Well, that's not true, but I wish I had a best friend I could do it with for practice. Someone I could trust.

Once, at one of my parents' parties, I was doing what I usually do, hanging in the pool house, watching a Western. Jackson came in, the son of one of my parents' friends. Home from college.

"Can I watch with you?" he asked, and I shrugged, though I was excited to have company. It was the summer before high school, and I was the only one of my group of friends who wasn't at tennis camp.

He handed me his glass of amber liquid, and I took a drink, then panted. It was like I had sipped fire.

"Try that again." He laughed, and I did, smoother that time.

He took the blanket I had and put it over himself so that we were sharing it, our legs out on the sectional couch. I couldn't focus on the movie, and when he took my hand under the blanket, I knew he wasn't focusing either. He put my hand over his pants and moved it back and forth, until I was doing it myself. Then he unzipped his pants, and I put my hand on his penis, but I didn't really know what to do or for how long, and shouldn't we be kissing? I stopped, and he looked at me and laughed, then got up and stumbled out. I felt so gross, so clumsy and stupid, and when I finally got up and went outside, my parents and everyone were out on the patio, having a great time. I walked up to my mom, but she gave me that look, the one that says, *Not now*, and for some reason, my first thought was *I don't want to be like you. I want to be tougher. I want to be cold.*

"So they're honored we chose them?" Jay says.

"A polite lie, I guess." Something my mom does a lot when she needs something.

He puts on his snowboard boots, but leaves them unlaced, and I put the book back on the shelf.

"Hey, can you go to Nicole's work?" he asks. "Skip just texted. She forgot to leave a change of clothes in her office. He asked if we could take her stuff to her. Since I doubt you have any plans, can you do it? Take the shuttle. Explore your surroundings." He spreads his arms apart, presenting me with all the possibilities, then heads to the door.

"Where do I go?"

"The Lodge and Spa." He pats his pockets, grabs his goggles off the hook by the door. "Skip said you go up Overlook until you see . . . it. Okay? Okay." He leaves, highlighting my solitude.

How does he already have plans in a new place? How is he so comfortable? I reattempt the sex move, widening my stance and scooping the air with my pelvis. I'd do me. So there.

I take the shuttle down Main Street, which lasts a second. What do people do in this town? The buildings look fake—like we're on a studio lot. I'm the only one on the bus not wearing ski clothes, and the passengers seem to be holding their gear as if they're angry with it. At the end of town the shuttle stops and everyone gets out. I stay on, and the driver moves past the last hotel and then up Overlook. Up and up and up. It's quite nice, this view. It reminds me of home, being up on the mountain and looking down, as if leaving everything behind. My aunt and uncle should have built a house up here. It's then that I remember she ran up this damn hill. Holy moly, no wonder. A baby probably couldn't hold on.

I walk into the hotel with Nicole's things and go to check-in, hoping I get the better-looking guy to wave me forward. That doesn't happen. I get the skinny dude with the pit bull ears.

"I'm looking for Nicole Town," I say.

"She's in guest services," he says. "Her office is right down that hall, past the checkers table. Or chess. Not sure."

"Thanks." I smile, but too much, since this made him happy and confident.

"We should play sometime," he says as I'm walking away. "Checkers. Or chess."

I fake laugh. "Sounds horrible," I mumble. If I were in a movie, I'd say it real loud.

I knock on her door even though it's open. She's standing up while talking on the phone, but gestures for me to come in.

"Tell them the sledding package is just as amazing." She rolls her eyes. "They don't need the bonuses. Make cocoa at home. Hey, my niece is here, so I should . . . What? No, it's fine. . . ."

She glances at me. I look around her office: books on resort tourism, framed pictures of trees and wolves.

"Not sure," she says, "and she's right here, so . . . anyway. No, I don't mind. I love the twins. Okay. . . . That's so funny, all right. . . . Well, I'll let you go. . . . That works! Okay, buh-bye— uh-huh, uh-huh, perfect. Okay. Talk to you later!"

She hangs up and sighs. "I swear you think you're almost to the end of the conversation, then bam! She hits you again." She plops down onto her chair.

"I can't believe you ran up that hill," I say.

"Yeah," she says, as if understanding it was crazy. "It helps me sleep."

"God," I say. "So would Scotch or an Ambien." Saying this makes me miss my dad. He always has a Scotch with his cherished ice cubes. My dad has some pretty cool things, but I've never heard him rave about his cars or toys the way he raves about his gourmet ice maker and top-hat ice.

"You need to use the cleanest, purest, most elegant cubes," he told me in the downstairs den, then made me examine the ice in his glass. "They won't alter the flavor or water down the Scotch. They're perfection. Why age something so perfectly, then destroy it?"

Nicole moves her bangs out of her eyes while typing. She

could use a Scotch with some excellent ice cubes. Except those ice machines are ten grand. It's crazy my dad would spend so much on something like that. Even though people chose to invest, I feel a little guilty that his—that *our*—lifestyle isn't dependent on their loss, but still good in spite of it. Though isn't that what business is about? We're in it too—probably lost a lot alongside everyone else. You work so hard to build something. If it doesn't pan out, that's unfortunate, but you put yourself in a position where you don't lose it all. You're smart. And when others aren't as smart, you don't just tear it all down. Why age something so perfectly, then destroy it?

"What was she saying about me?" I ask. Nicole was clearly talking about me with whoever was on the phone.

"Who?" She doesn't look up.

"The person you were talking to on the phone."

She stops typing. "Tanya? Oh, just . . ." She holds her hands together and looks at her fingers. "She said you must be having a hard time seeing your father behave so unethically."

"Wow."

"I'm honest when asked direct questions. I don't want to be, but I have trouble lying. It never comes off right. But neither does the truth, obviously. Sorry. People are kind of pissed at your dad right now."

"I don't know why," I say. "People make their own choices. I happen to believe in him."

"Of course, I—"

"He can't control the real estate market. People need to be responsible for themselves." My heart quickens. I feel like I'm in a courtroom defending myself.

Nicole just nods, seeming to know I'm reciting something I don't fully understand.

"I thought you were supposed to hide our identities." I smirk.

"Yeah, I guess I told Tanya you were coming before I got your mom's memo. And Skip is a little more into that than I am. Why hide is what I say."

"Here." I walk to her desk to hand over her things.

"Oh gosh, thank you." She walks around the desk. "I have a black garment bag. I guess Skip forgot to tell you."

Something drops, and I reach to pick it up. The item happens to be big purple panties, which don't seem to be the best choice as far as baby making goes.

"Next time I'll bring the bag," I say.

She balls the underwear up and makes them disappear.

"Not like there will be a next time," she says. "I mean, you don't have to bring my things up here. I usually have spare clothes."

I walk toward the window to look at the mountain range. I feel her looking at me.

"You're so . . . dressed up," she says. "You going somewhere?"

I look down at my outfit. Brown knee-high leather boots, a fitted sweater, and a suit jacket with suede patches on the elbows. Not really a big deal.

"I'm just wearing jeans," I say.

"You just look so adult," she says. "Professional."

I shrug. It's a pretty basic outfit. "So what do you do?" I ask, turning to face her.

"Guest relations," she says. "I'm a concierge, pretty much. I design packages for the guests. Help them organize their days, book experiences. People don't know what to do with themselves. Or they know exactly what to do and what they want, and I scramble to make it happen. People are pretty chill here, though. It's not like Vail or Aspen. More about keeping the kids squared away."

I go back to the desk and sit down like a client, and she follows suit and sits down.

I imagine visitors doing various things: an awkward teen learning to "pizza" at his ski lesson, a couple dogsledding, kids tubing, a woman getting a massage at a spa.

"They get nervous they're not making the right choices," she says. "So I tell them how to spend their money, which costs money."

I look at her desk. My dad's home desk has outdated pictures of us. It's kind of weird when people don't have kids. Do you put pictures of your husband up? Your cat? Some wildflowers? She has no pictures. I can feel her watching me, checking out her life through my eyes.

"Didn't you work somewhere else when I was young?" I ask.

"Yup. As a waitress. Your mom, too, before she had you. I convinced her to move here with me after I graduated from CU. I met a dishwasher—Skip—and she met your dad." She laughs to herself. "We had fun. Your parents partied."

"Really?"

She's remembering something. Her face is relaxed and full of warmth.

"They were fun. They were nice." She continues to gaze off into Memory Town.

I've always liked hearing stories about my parents and about myself when I was young. There's something comforting in knowing you've done something worth remembering, or that someone took the time to craft a scene for you. Also, the things you did to bother people sort of become what you're fondly known for later on. I like hearing about my parents, considering all the life that existed before me.

"Your parents have changed so much," Nicole says, her gaze still far off, but then she comes to. "Us, not so much." She furrows her brow, then types something into her computer.

"So what experience should I have today?" I ask.

She looks toward the window. "You could ski, I guess."

"That's what you'd say? Fired."

She smiles, but not too much, which I like. She's not like other adults, who act like everything you say is funny or interesting, or who ask too many questions about school and hobbies.

"Okay—if you were really a guest, I'd first get to know you." She lets her hair out of her rubber band. It's a stylish, longish bob, and this paired with her high cheekbones makes her look sort of posh.

"I'd do a kind of interview. I'd ask what you like, what you want to get away from. We'd think of things you could do here that you couldn't do anywhere else."

"How do you keep the kids squared away?" I ask.

"First I ask the parents what their kids like, what they're afraid of. We think of things to occupy the children so the parents feel okay about leaving them."

"So what did you and my parents come up with to occupy us?"

"You're a funny one," she says.

"I use humor to mask my pain. Kidding."

"Me too," she says.

I lean in and squint. "Look at your eyebrows."

"Now, how am I supposed to do that?" she says.

Her brows are dark and thick and perfectly uniform except the little curl on the end. "You have rogue eyebrow hairs on the left."

"Oh yeah, I forgot to trim them. Only on the left side—the weirdest thing."

"Jay has the exact same thing. Except he wouldn't think of trimming them. He's not really a grooming type."

She touches her eyebrow and looks down, and I worry I've made her self-conscious. She then stammers, "Is it h-hard?"

"His eyebrows?"

"No," she says. "Having a sibling who's so different from you."

"Sometimes," I say. "Do you mean because he's likable and I'm not?"

"That's not what I meant." Nicole looks back at her computer and begins to type quickly. "I was just thinking about me and your mom."

"Who was the likable one?" I ask.

Nicole stops typing. "I think you know the answer to that."

I don't think it's hard to be the less likable. Not when it's my choice. Maybe I work at it—being unliked, being feared. Maybe I reject everything or everyone who wouldn't have me anyway. My brother can look stupid with no consequence.

"What happened to you guys?" I ask. "To you and my mom."

She looks up at me, and I think she's deciding how much to say. Something had to have happened, and yet how bad could it be if we're staying with them now?

"I don't even know anymore," she says. "We don't get along." She looks up. "Until she needs me."

"Did something specific happen?" I ask.

Nicole smiles to herself and shakes her head. "Maybe a whole bunch of specifics. It's her story to tell."

"Well, then," I say. "I'll let you get to it."

"I'll see you at home," she says, which sounds so strange. "One sec," she says before I walk out the door. I hear a printer hum. She reaches under her desk, then hands me a piece of paper. "Thanks again for bringing my things."

I leave, even more determined to figure out what happened between them.

7

I catch a shuttle back to town and look at ANNIE'S ITINERARY designed by Nicole Town, Guest Concierge. At the top: TUBING.

There's no way I'm going tubing by myself, and while the Barney Ford House Museum looks interesting—he was an escaped slave who became a famous entrepreneur and a civil rights pioneer—I don't feel like nerding out right now.

The shuttle ride feels different going back down. I'm more sure of myself and have warmed up to the vibe of this place. Colorful buildings, homey, people in comfortable clothes, cinnamon-scented air.

I get out at the first stop and walk—bumps of ice on the sidewalk, wreath-wrapped streetlights. Music blasts out of the burger place, and I pet a gray-and-white dog that's tied up outside of a coffee shop. I let him smell my hand first, rub the soft fur between his ears, then look at the name tag: BOB BARKER. I'm in love.

Everyone around me seems to be in love as well, or to be celebrating something. Celebrating fun, friends, the fact that their family isn't being scrutinized. Rejoicing in fathers who aren't being demonized. The sun is dazzling, the air chilled, and when I notice a group of people my age looking at me, I smile, feeling a little smug, until I really take them in and realize Nicole's right. I look strange to them. Overdressed. Someone not their age, irrelevant. I get the urge to fix it.

The stores on this side of the street are in two-level clusters. Some shops are around a little bend, sunken like deep pockets. I step into a boutique called Canary in a Clothes Mine and browse the too-cute clothes, most of which you wouldn't really wear here at this time of year, or ever. The clothes smell like hot irons and wildflowers. The music is loud, which makes me feel like buying things even more. I touch the garments and put on a face like I'm considering something far more important. A mom and daughter are browsing next to me, so I can hear everything they say, which isn't much, just a lot of "This is cute." "So cute." "Super cute."

I browse the rack, and for the first time I'm sorta glad I'm here. Why not make the best of it? At the bottom of Nicole's itinerary for me, she wrote *Be yourself (or whoever you'd like to be)*. Even my attempts at casual wear can come off overly polished, like I'm dressing for an interview. Be who I would like to be? Well, I like these clothes. I'm Annie Town, and this is what she'd wear. I take off my stiff jacket and tie it around my waist.

"Can I get the vest?" the daughter asks. She has long straight hair with bangs and looks like a folk singer.

"How much is it?" the mom asks.

"One seventy-five?" the daughter says, and uses an expression that is highly familiar—a cringing, cute face that harkens back to baby days, which are long gone. It works every time with my mom, and my dad never even asks how much things are. He just hands over the card.

"Absolutely not," the mom says. "For that? It doesn't even have sleeves."

"Mom, come on, just—"

"You have an allowance." The mom continues to flip through clothes, done.

The girl puts the vest back. That's it? I would have pushed it a little further. I pick up the vest—it is cute—along with a pair of high-waisted jeans, a cable-knit sweater, and a few of the same shirts in different colors. I choose clothes for my new self—I will be a sexy, trendy, cute girl now. I will wear fringe and look festival-ready. The shopgirl, who is wearing these great lightning bolt earrings, offers to take my things, freeing my hands for more. I go up to the girl who wanted the vest, something I'd never have done before.

"Sucks about the vest," I say.

She rolls her eyes. "I know, right?"

She's pretty, with dark skin and long lashes.

"Next time ask for something more expensive and have what you really want as backup. Then it looks like you're making a generous compromise."

She smiles. "That's funny."

"Then try it on and say that it just makes you feel so confident, like you'll fit in. Moms can't help but want their daughters to avoid social problems."

"Thanks," she says. "I'll try."

When I'm done in the dressing room, I walk to the counter and get rung up. There are handmade soaps and candles at the counter, so I add some of them to the pile because they'd make good gifts. My mom has a closet full of gifts for friends, housekeepers, etc.

I hand over my credit card to the older lady at the register. She looks at my card, then at me, and I open my wallet to get my license, since she's going to be all skeptical.

"You related to Jacob Tripp?" she asks, and the question startles me. She has a gray bun and black-framed eyeglasses. She doesn't seem like a trendy boutique type, but maybe she owns the shop or makes the soap. She looks like a soap maker.

I've been asked if I'm related to Jacob Tripp before, but something tells me she's not asking out of admiration. So this is what my parents were talking about. We really do need to hide and chuck our last name, and this realization gives me a shock of shame. My normal self would talk back, own it, and be defensive, but now I just say, in a cool-girl, teen voice, "What? Who?"

"Jacob Tripp. The developer," she says, folding my jeans. "The one in the news."

"Um, no?" I say, and this makes me feel guilty and sad.

"He really messed up some lives," she says. "Screwed over my friend's stepsister."

She sounds funny. I took her for an artsy hippie, but she sounds like she should work in a real coal mine. Maybe she's the canary.

"Never heard of him," I say. "I must be part of another Tripp lineage. We're from Chattanooga." I sign the receipt, not looking at the total, then get the hell out of there, feeling like I've stolen something. What would she have said if I'd told her I was his daughter? Chase me out of the store with soap? Lecture me? I almost want to yell at her. It's not like I've done anything wrong, and if her friend's stepsister—or whoever—invested, she was probably rich to begin with, and rich people take risks, take losses. It's part of the game. But I know how bad that would sound, and for the first time I'm realizing that I don't know what game my dad is involved in. For the first time I feel like I'm on the wrong side.

On Main Street I walk with my head down, breathing hard. Damn this high altitude. I'm dizzy. I need water. I need to acclimate to this height, to this life. I spot an ATM across the street. I don't want to use my card again, don't want to feel this way again. I withdraw just three hundred. My hands shake, and my face is hot.

"Annie," I hear, and look up to see Jay walking from the gondola with his board. His goggles are pushed up on his forehead.

"Snow's no good," he says. "Want a lift home?"

"Yeah," I say. "Home home."

"What did you buy?" he asks as we walk down Main.

"Clothes," I say. "Frickin' soap."

Stuff I don't even know if we can afford anymore. Jay carries his board behind him so it sometimes hits my back. I've always felt good walking with my brother, something I'd never admit to him even if he was dying.

"I miss Mom and Dad and Sammy," I say when I look into a shop and see a family eating lunch.

I expect ridicule, but instead he says, "I know."

I hand him the itinerary. He looks it over and laughs, and then we walk to his car and go to the home that's not ours, filled with the strangers we know.

8

It's freezing out, and yet here we are, in the backyard at night, waiting while Nicole stages the dinner table and Skip sets up Skype. Everyone looks blue. I pull my beanie down over my ears and think of the people who believe my dad has deceived them. I wish they could know the real him, and then hope that all I feel I know about him is true.

"I followed it to a tee," Jay says to Nicole. He's talking about my itinerary. He's so damn pleasant. When we got home, he went out and did all the things I was supposed to do, while I stayed in my room and tried on clothes. I imagine him at the top of a hill with an inner tube, waiting his turn to fly down, and I'm filled with envy and a deep admiration.

"You did *not* do everything," Nicole says, laughter blooming from her.

"I did!" Jay says.

Nicole folds a napkin and places a fork on it. "Even the museum?"

"Yup," Jay says, then follows her rhythm, folding a napkin, placing a fork on it. I could help, but I want to keep my seat warm.

"Barney, the black baron of Colorado." He holds a fork in the air. "Escaped slavery on the Underground Railroad. Became a hotel and restaurant tycoon. Really interesting man." He continues around the table. "Then I went on the sleigh ride. Annie, you gotta go. People were singing. It was hilarious."

"Annie, what did you do today?" Skip asks, exchanging a look with Nicole.

I try to include everything so I sound just as adventurous. "I took the shuttle up to the lodge, then walked around town. Made you guys dinner. Bought this vest." I twist one of the buttons.

"That's great," Skip says. "Glad you guys had such great days."

"What is that, caribou?" Jay asks.

"No." I glance down at the vest.

"Are you a furry now?"

"I could shoot you in between the eyes, asshole."

Nicole laughs.

Skip says, "Whoa," and then, "Okay, I got it to dial."

"Why are we out here?" I ask.

"Best connection," Skip says.

"That's odd," I say.

"Come on over. Hon, it's dialing, but I need to get to work, so I'll just duck out—"

"Everyone sit down!" Nicole says. "Get close." I walk over slowly and sit down next to her.

Skip kisses her on the head, but she takes his hand, holding him still. "Just stay for a sec, please," she says, and begins to serve the salad to the plate in front of me. When my mom comes up on screen, Nicole acts like it's a big surprise.

"Oh, hi!" she says. "We're all just eating dinner together. Annie made it for us. She's been cooking up a storm."

My mom looks like she's in space. "Hi, Mom," I say. "The screen's so dirty," I say to Nicole.

"Hi, honey," my mom says. "Hi, Jay. How are you guys?"

"Good," we both say. Jay stands in back of me.

"Yeah, real good," Jay says. "Fun day. I did stuff. Annie bought stuff. The usual."

My mom just sits there smiling, and I wonder if she heard. I feel like I'm talking to a news reporter in Syria.

"I needed some essentials," I say, wanting to see if she'll tell me that we shouldn't be spending money.

"Oh, good," she says, not revealing anything. "I want it to be livable, for you to feel comfortable and—"

"It's perfectly livable," Nicole says lightly, but her jaw is set hard.

"Where's Dad?" I ask. Jay sits down next to me.

"He's just finishing a call," my mom says. "Jay, your elbows."

Jay takes his elbows off the table, as if that matters right now.

"This whole Skype thing," my mom says. "I can't see—"

"It's like she's looking over our heads," I say.

"How did everything go today?" Nicole asks.

"Kids." My dad enters the picture, patting his forehead with a cloth. He looks like he's floating, even when he eventually sits down. His forehead is red and sweaty. His face comes real close and then drops back. It's like they're talking to us from space. I can't really read their expressions.

"Dad," Jay says, "what's going on? Can I help with anything on this end?"

"Hey, guys, sorry," Skip says. "I've really got to run, but catch me up when I get home."

"Still working nights, huh?" my dad says.

"Yup, since it's a restaurant."

"Good for you," my dad says. "This world needs people like you."

"Right. Thanks." Skip awkwardly kisses Nicole good-bye, and you can tell they probably don't normally kiss each other good-bye. Everyone waits for him to leave before continuing.

"How did today go?" I ask.

"Just like we expected," my dad says. "We did really, really well."

"Will that mean people like Joanie aren't going to lose their money?" I ask. "What are they saying?"

"It's complex," my dad says after a long beat. Probably the connection.

"Can we be at court?" I ask. "That may help—to show people you have a family?"

"That's sweet," he says, as if I've said something charming instead of strategic.

"I bought some clothes today," I say, "but switched to cash after the clerk asked if I was related to you."

Not so charming. Everyone is silent. Jay clears his throat.

"This is why I said to keep a low profile," my mom says, her voice rising, as if I'm the one who has done something wrong.

My dad places his hand on her shoulder, and she flinches. "I'm sorry that happened," he says. "I'm sorry for anyone who's hurting right now. That's why I'm here. Defending myself and the other investors who gave it their best shot."

He looks down, and I feel bad for making him think about more than he needs to right now.

"It's good to see you guys doing okay under the circumstances," my mom says. Her gaze drifts off behind us. "We'll let you get back to your dinner. Are you outside? Isn't it cold?"

"They're fine," Nicole says. "There's a heat lamp."

My dad looks at his phone. "We'll talk again."

"Why would Cee's dad be testifying?" I ask before he can go. "He's your partner, basically."

My dad looks up from his phone. "He just . . . There's been a little confusion over a consulting company we've been using out in Delaware." He gives me a smile. "Don't worry about it. We'll get it cleared up. Look. Let's check in after tomorrow, okay?"

"Bye, kids," my mom says.

Nicole disconnects before proper farewells and looks at me and Jay like she feels sorry for us and pissed at them, or maybe it's the other way around. We start to eat. Jay puts his elbows back on the table.

I chew the cold salad, feeling useless, wishing I could do something to help.

"It's frickin' freezing out here," Nicole says. "Let's go in."

I help Nicole clean up the kitchen, something I never do, but find that I don't mind doing it. It's like meditation or tai chi—circles with the sponge, running my hands through water.

Jay walks out of his room. He's wearing a collared shirt and jeans.

"I'm heading out, if that's cool."

Nicole looks up from the sink. "What's your curfew?"

"I'm free-range," he says.

She looks at me as if for confirmation, and I raise my eyebrows. "Yup."

"I wish your mother had told me what you're allowed and not allowed to do," she says.

"You could just ask me," he says, and puts on his jacket.

"I want to go," I say, and run my hand through my hair.

"Yeah," he says, as though I'm being sarcastic, and he turns toward the door.

"I really do," I say. I want to get out of here. I want to do something new.

"Go on," Nicole says. "Take your sister."

I look at her, surprised.

"Her curfew's eleven," Jay says.

Nicole's brow furrows. "And you have no curfew? That's not fair. You guys be home by midnight together."

I tuck in my lips to hold down a smile, then I throw a clean, wet wooden spoon at him, which hits him on the back. "Ow," he says. He picks it up and whips it back to me, but I catch it like a badass.

"Wow," he says. "Good one."

"Where are you going, anyway?" Nicole asks.

"Meeting some friends to play pool." He bounces on his heels. "Joffrey and Eric," he says to me.

"They're coming all the way here for you?" I ask, and wish I hadn't.

"Yup," he says. "Let's go, then."

We go to a bar called Cecilia's and somehow get in because Eric knows the bouncer. His parents have a condo in Breckenridge, and I guess he comes here a lot. The place is thumping with pop hip-hop, the kind of music that makes it okay for girls to dance all slutty while making pouty kissy faces. That's what they're doing out there on the dance floor, and instead of judging them, I'm glad I bought clothes today that help me blend in. My vest doesn't make me look like a furry, and my fitted jeans are on point. Even Eric and Joffrey do a double take.

I watch them play pool while scoping things out.

Joffrey, a tall, skinny dude, is scoping things out, too, while chalking his stick.

"This place is D-bag central," he says. "And I'm the only black dude here. Or ethnic dude, even. Or wait, I see an Asian dude, but that doesn't count."

"Dude, you're always the only black guy," my brother says. "You love it. This place is kind of lame, though."

"So what?" Eric says. "Bunch of hotties up in here."

They all look at the table next to them, where a girl is smoking a cigar, really sucking and doing up the phallic symbol of it, as if to say, *One day this could be you.*

"I can get into it," Joffrey says.

Eew.

"Speaking of things I can get into," he says. "I'll take care of Sadie while you're gone. I'll eat her snacks. Why's she always bringing people snacks?"

"She wants to be loved," my brother says. "And they're good snacks."

"She's been moping around," Eric says. "It's like you've gone to war. I'm going to tell her you went to war, then I'll comfort the shit out of her."

My brother leans over the table to line up his next shot, ignoring them.

"You guys are like scholarship kids," Joffrey says. "You live all far."

"Buy the next round, then," I say, and they all turn to look at me like they forgot I was here.

"I think you guys should buy," Eric says. "Since your dad seemed to make it out just in time."

"Snap," Joffrey says, snapping his fingers then taking his shot.

"What?" Eric says. "Too soon?"

"Way too soon," Joffrey says, but he's speaking lightly, I notice, whereas there's a dark glimmer in Eric's eye, an iciness in his tone.

"What are you talking about?" my brother says, his voice calm and similar to Joffrey's.

"Just listening to my dad's shit," Eric says.

My eyes go back and forth between the three of them, not wanting to miss an expression or a secret glance.

"Can't blame a man for knowing when to pull out," Jay says, and takes his shot. He misses it—not the shot, but the exchange of glances between his friends. He moves by me to line up his next play, misses, and says, "And whatever, they're friends."

Eric stands there, not taking his turn. "Dude. My dad invested in his shit. They're not friends anymore."

My brother shrugs, but he's clearly annoyed. "Whatever, it'll work out." I can tell he's undone by confrontation, both ashamed and defensive of our family as I was earlier today at the store.

After two shots of something wicked Joffrey foisted upon

me, I head out to the dance floor with the boys, and we dance ironically to Biggie. But as the songs go on, I find myself just dancing and being a good listener—I obey the lyrics by bending my knees, touching the floor, and getting low. At one point I even grab a shorty and make my pelvis act like a ladle against his thigh. I shake my head so my hair whips my face.

"What's your name!" the guy I'm dancing with yells.

"Scotch!" I yell, since I taste it in my mouth.

"Scott?"

"Scotch! Scotch Mizutani!"

He smiles, then gives me a questioning look and presses my lower back into him. I don't think he heard. I don't think he cares. He's not even very attractive, I realize. I mean, he's handsome, but in this highly crafted way. I can smell the gel in his hair. It's then that I take a closer look and think that maybe he looks a little older than I had thought. I look around for the boys, but don't see them anywhere. I feel a little dizzy now, and the boy—the man—gives me this hungry look, and the light on his face tells me, yes, he is old. He's really old, and I can feel his boner against me.

"I'm sixteen," I say.

"Even better," he whispers in my ear.

"I gotta go," I say, and walk away.

9

I hear Jay coming in. I wonder if he's even worried about me. I'm watching some strange movie that only plays at times like these. I hear him rummage in the kitchen, where I'm sure he's looking for something salty, and then I hear his steps. I both want and don't want him to come in and see me, because I've been crying and he can always tell. I think I hear him pause in front of my room. He pounds on my door, then opens it kind of sheepishly, guitar and a snack in hand.

"Where'd you go?" he asks.

"Where'd *you* go?" I ask.

"Nowhere," he says. "We were dancing, then went back to the bar. Joff said you were dancing with some dude." My brother laughs, but it seems fake somehow. "Everyone was all tripped out."

He walks to my bed and holds out the bag of chips. I've got my huge comforter over me and must look like a dead whale.

"Why were they tripped out?" I ask. "They couldn't believe someone actually found me attractive?"

"No, god, hardly that. It's just—you know, you're usually . . . uptight. Busy. No-access Annie. Don't be mad."

"I'm not mad! They're just wrong, that's all." I cross my arms over my chest. "No-access Annie? Is that a thing?"

"It's not a big deal," he says, which doesn't answer my question. "They were just surprised. It's not a bad thing. You're just not really a flirty-girly-dance-floor type. Chill. I hope you had fun."

He looks at me with a warm expression. The TV is loud—on it, the little girl is still crying because her dad yelled at her mom for lying to him about her job as a pole dancer.

"I thought it was you crying," Jay says, then squints at my face. I sniffle.

"Oh my god," he says. "Get it together."

"I was crying at the movie," I lie. Like I care that the mother isn't a stripper, she just wants to go to the pole dancing championships in Miami. She has found her passion. "I have empathy, okay? They're strong tears, I'm not wimpy crying—"

"Strong flow, got it."

"The guy I was dancing with was disgusting," I say. "I was trying to have fun, and . . . when I do, it always goes bad. I want to go home. I don't understand what's happening. I feel like Dad shouldn't be so confident. I know he's innocent, but other people don't seem to think so."

"You know how this goes. Dad's like a celebrity, you know? People want to see him go down."

"Like his friends? You heard Eric."

His face seems to close like a fist. "Yeah," he says. "I get the digs, I guess, but . . . I mean, they've got tons of money. It's not like Dad took it all away. Or any of it. I don't know."

He just tried to comfort me, yet doesn't seem convinced or comforted himself.

"I keep calling Cee," I say. "She won't call or text me back."

"Probably because her dad was the project manager," Jay says. "But if her dad had managed the project in the first place, we wouldn't be here."

"It's happening," I say. "Everyone's turning against us. At school. Cee. Just now at the bar. And Mom seemed like she's experiencing a lot of it."

Jay continues to play a folk song that always makes me want to go on a long drive with a boy at the wheel. The boy is rugged and cool. I'm all awesome, with marsala lipstick and my caramel Stetson hat, or forget that, no lipstick, 'cause we'll be on a dusty road and the dirt will stick to my mouth. I start to cry again. I can't help it.

"Oh, come on," Jay says, and I'm about to tell him I'm crying because I love this song, how it makes me think of campfires and starry skies and better times, but it's more than that, and I tell the truth:

"I just read an article about families with dads who go to jail, and like, everyone turns against them. Especially the moms. The mom is banished from the parties and clubs, and sometimes they have to sell their houses, and the dads work as laundry attendants in jail and make, like, ten bucks a week instead of ten million a year."

"Easy there, tiger," Jay says. "You're talking about dads who've been convicted, and who've done, like, Ponzi schemes. Big stuff. Dad's not going to be convicted. And he didn't purposefully try to scheme people out of their money, okay? That's the difference." He picks the strings. His face is pinched.

I realize I've been holding my breath and let it out. "Do you know that for sure?" I ask.

I hear someone coming down the hallway, and we both freeze and look at one another.

Uncle Skip peeks in. He's red-nosed from the cold. "Hey, guys. Everything okay?"

"Annie's depressed," Jay says.

"And you're not?" I sit up and check to see if my pajamas are covering me sufficiently.

"She needs to do something she can't do anywhere else," Jay says. He pats my back.

"God, shut up, vermin." I roll my shoulders to shake him off.

"See?" he says. "It's serious."

Skip walks in. He runs his hand through his thick brown hair and sits on the edge of the bed. I pull up the covers, mortified. Skip reaches into the bag of chips.

"These will be my demise," he says, then looks at me like I've just run into a wall. "It's totally understandable that you miss home. And that you're worried about things. Tonight on the phone . . . that must have been difficult."

I just nod, and Skip nods back like we're agreeing on something. Maybe I have run into a wall. He eats another chip and seems to be really tasting it, trying to identify the ingredients.

"Come work at Steak and Rib." He looks so eager and pure. "I need a server. You could do it for the rest of break—what's that, two weeks? And when school starts up, you could come in after school? Or . . . you probably have homework. Or you won't be here."

Week and a half. I've been counting the days. And then I won't be here. Our dad will win, and I won't need a job.

"If we're still here, she can work weekends," Jay says, also munching on chips. "She doesn't do shit on weekends but skate, and that's all done. Hey, these aren't bad." He reads the bag. "Potatoes, flax, sea salt, all organic."

"What do you think?" Skip says to me.

I bring my knees up to my chest. I think I'd like everyone to leave my room now. "Servers have to talk to people," I say.

"Yeah, she sucks at that," Jay says, and makes a loud pluck on the guitar.

"What about the kitchen?" Skip says as if his idea is the key to my heart. "You love cooking! I mean, you wouldn't be cooking, but . . . you'd be around it. You could see what happens. I could start you off tomorrow. Then you could work New Year's Eve after that. Bang!"

The bed bounces.

"Bang!" Jay says. "And you knows you gots no plans."

Something about this whole thing actually appeals to me. I imagine being in an apron, dicing, mixing, a mean chef reluctantly nodding his approval. I'd rise to the top fast, wowing everyone by adding that one special spice that drops jaws. I'd be introduced as Annie Town. I could be whoever I wanted to be. A flirty dancing girl. A girl no one would be surprised to see having fun. A girl who doesn't think so much. All-access Annie. But without the porn vibe.

"Okay," I say. "Until we leave. So, not for long."

Jay strums on his guitar, one big finale-like sound, like we have all accomplished something tremendous together. Then he gets up, and so does Skip.

"Great," Skip says. "It will take your mind off things. Keep you busy."

I pull the covers up, waiting for them to leave. Jay walks out, and Skip follows.

"Good night," he says.

"Good night," I say.

He closes the door, and I lie back down. This is good. Tomorrow I'll truly start as Annie Town.

10

The next morning, day two, I get a text from Cee that must have come overnight.

What do you want?

What do I want? For you to answer my damn texts!

What's up with you? I write, and feel like I should be more specific so she can't just say, "Nothing."

I'm living in Breck with my aunt and uncle. Can you talk? I know our dads have drama, but we don't

I sit on the bed and wait for a while, then give up and get dressed, opting for one of my new shirts and strategically ripped jeans.

I walk out to the living room, and Nicole is standing behind the couch with her leg propped on a cushion in a balletic stretch. When she sees me, she shuts the TV off, but it's too late. I caught a glimpse of my dad. I recognized the shirt first, one I helped him order online from Nordstrom. Dark brown. Reminded me of something a banker in the seventies would wear. I thought it would look great with a pink tie.

"Turn it back on," I say. "Please."

She puts her leg down and points the remote at the television.

I catch the back of him walking into the courthouse and the reporter signing off, moving on to traffic and weather.

"What did they say?" I ask.

"They just repeated the charges of, uh . . . real estate fraud, then showed him walking in. He looked confident, but not cocky, so that's good." She gives me an apologetic look, then turns it off again.

"Oh," I say. Real estate fraud. That word *fraud* sounds so awful.

She puts her other leg up to stretch. "So I hear you're going to work in the kitchen today?"

"Yeah," I say. She looks amused and skeptical.

"Want an omelet?" I ask, knowing she'll say no.

"No, thanks," she says. "Running to work. You going to do anything from the itinerary today?"

"Maybe," I say.

"You don't need to go in until three," she says. "That gives you plenty of time to get out there."

She looks at the dark TV, then back at me as if knowing I'm waiting for her to leave so I can turn it on again. "There's nothing you can do," she says.

"I know."

When she leaves, I have breakfast, then go back to my room. I look at my phone on the bed, and there's a text from Cee:

My dad's going to testify against your dad.

I know, I text back. **My dad told me about the confusion. What does your dad think?** I ask, trying to get their side. When my dad explained he's testifying over some confusion about a consulting company, I pretended to understand better than I do.

I see the dots appear, then retract.

Jesus, she writes. **Get a clue.**

Yes, Cee, I think to myself. *That's exactly what I'm trying to do.*

The Steak and Rib kitchen is loud and male-dominant, and I feel a heat pour through my body and my hands shake a bit.

Skip whistles, and everyone looks up. I give a timid little smile, but then I remember this is my chance. I stand tall, eye the place with a smirk and a confidence, then realize this is something Annie Tripp would do, and so I try to give off warm, friendly vibes.

"Guys, this is my niece, Annie. Annie Town." He looks at me with an apologetic grin.

"Hey," I say, and the guys nod.

"Pablo and Ren," he says, pointing to the guys by the sinks. "Freddie—head chef. Brose—where's Brose?"

"Not here yet," Freddie says. "We're good, though."

Brose? I think to myself. *What kind of name is that?*

"Forest . . ."

"Over here," Forest says, coming out of some back area. Forest looks like he's not entirely sober.

"Hi, I'm Annie," I say.

"What?" he asks.

"Nothing, Forest." Skip shakes his head. "Guys, introduce her to the waitstaff as they come in. Ren, have her shadow you guys." He puts his hand on my shoulder. "You going to be okay? It's just dishes. I need to get out front."

"Yeah," I say. "I'll be fine."

I follow Ren around for a while until he gives me my own

task—loading dusty potatoes into the dishwasher. I've never heard of doing this and hope I'm not misunderstanding.

"Like this?" I ask, gesturing to the potato I place in the rack.

"Yeah, yeah," he says, impatient. "Rinse. No soap."

I continue, avoiding eye contact with anyone, but watch them when I can. They're all incredibly busy and seem angry about it, and whenever I don't have something to do I feel huge and clumsy in the small space, like an elephant in a porta potty. I thought I could be friendly, cool, and confident, but it's another country in here, and I don't know the language. After I've finished loading the potatoes, I walk over to Ren, the only person here I feel at ease with, perhaps because he's a lot older and he's sort of in charge of me.

"Can I help?" I ask, looking at the counter covered with shrimp.

He moves some shrimp my way, then gestures for me to follow what he does. He does one slowly, going through each step, then goes back to his utterly fast rhythm. It's like watching someone shuffle. I take a shrimp, remove the head and feet, pull off the shell, then make a slit with my knife down the middle of the shrimp's back. He gestures to the bag where he's been saving the remnants.

"Fish stock," he says.

I do a few more and am overwhelmed when I look at the rest of the pile. At least music is playing, but I wish we could have a little more fun.

I hold up a vein. "So weird this is the whole digestive tract," I say. Ren looks at it, and I can't tell if he understands. "Colon, stomach," I say.

"Poop," he says.

"Right."

A waiter comes through the swinging door carrying a plate full of food and looking peeved. I've heard the guys call him Nat, and the girls, Natty. He's cute, and seems to know this about himself.

"She says it's not done," he says to Brose, who came in about a half hour ago. He's the line cook and is always grimacing, never still, yet there's a kind of grace in his flurry. With his name, I expected some overly cool bros-before-hos type, but he seems a bit uptight, despite his looks—a little scruffy, like someone who's into camping. He's the only one here who has yet to say hello or even recognize my existence.

He looks at the plate that Nat places in front of him, then he looks up at the order.

"It says medium rare," he says, shaking the pan. The mushrooms jump and sizzle. "That's medium rare. It's perfect, actually. Gorgeous color."

"She said the pinkness made her think of the ostrich," Nat says.

"Hell, she should think of the ostrich," Brose says. "It's what she's gonna eat."

I bite my lip, holding down a smile, perhaps to participate somehow.

"She made her choice," Brose says.

"She needs to commit," I say, which makes my heart beat as I pull poop.

Finally, he looks at me, then quickly away as if I had interrupted. Tough crowd. I go back to tearing off tails.

"I'll put it back on and ruin it," I hear Brose say, and then Nat

83

says, "I don't know you yet," and I look up. He has a friendly, playful smile. His hair, short and neat. Intense blue eyes. Not the camping type. More the type I was dancing with the other night—clean, groomed, skier-boy, but young.

"I'm Nat," he says.

He looks like if I poked him in the stomach, it would hurt my finger.

"I'm A-Annie," I stutter. "I'll be your dishwasher tonight."

"What's that?" he says.

"Nothing," I say. "Just, I'm dish washing. I'm a dishwasher and a shrimp detailer, poop puller." Oh my god. That just happened. Brose raises his eyebrows, but I can tell that whatever I've said earned me points somehow.

"You're the best-looking dishwasher I've ever seen," Natty says. "No offense, Ren."

I catch Brose rolling his eyes, and I think Pablo is translating what Nat just said to Ren, who shrugs as though conceding my ranking. I accidentally drop a shrimp, pick it up, set it back on the counter, look at Ren, then throw it away. I've never been this klutzy before. Is it from Nat's gaze or from being new, not just to this kitchen, but to work itself? I wasn't this awkward when Nat wasn't here, though. I'm used to boys like Nat, but this feels different because I'm different. He doesn't know me, doesn't think I'm an uptight priss. I'm hot versus distant and antisocial. I'm surmountable. I smile at him and feel my face burn, and while there's some benefit to him not knowing me, I wish I looked as I normally do, put together, like him.

"Here," Brose says to Nat, pushing the plate toward him. The meat, once tender, is now rock-ish. "Well done," he says. "What a waste."

I give Brose a look of knowing—it *is* a waste, and it says a lot about the consumer. She probably puts ketchup on it, too. I almost say this, but Brose returns my look with one that says, *What are you looking at?*

I return his hostility, mirroring his expression. What's his problem? I guess I know. He must see through my act. He must see the privileged girl stopping in for a little life experience. Guys like him never give me the time of day. I suppose they're as judgmental of girls like me as girls like me are of them.

Now that dinner service is almost over, I'm back to dishes, which are stacking up at an overwhelming rate. A waitress walks in with a tray of shots, and the kitchen staff gather around her and throw 'em back, not in some celebratory way, but more like they're running a race and the shots are little cups of water. She's come in before, and there's an air of assuredness about her—like it's some territory she's taken over, and she's running the show.

The girl comes up to me. She has short hair with long bangs, green eyes, and notably full lips.

"You've got quite a pile there," she says.

I look at my mounting load of dishes and stand up straighter.

"Here," she says, and hands me a glass of amber liquid. I take the shot and make a face, which probably looked like I had sucked a lemon. She watches the production with amusement, like she gave it to me just to be entertained.

"You're Skip's niece," she says.

"I am," I say, my eyes watering. "Absolutely. Annie Town."

"Absolutely Annie Town." She smirks. "I'm Rickie. Skip told me not to give you any shots, and he told me to be your friend."

I load a plate into the rack. Something in me releases, and I'm warm. Poised. I'm a carefree girl with self-possession. I occupy myself well, too.

"You don't have to be my friend," I say, "but you can keep the shots comin'."

"Ha!" she says, and I reflexively smile at her huge, consuming grin. She turns to leave. "Good job, boys!" she says, and Pablo drops down another load in front of me.

The kitchen is even louder, but more relaxed now that dinner is over. People are singing, and I don't feel like such an elephant. In an odd way, I feel like I belong. It's a sensation I don't get a lot, even while skating on a team. I'd keep to myself, always competing. I wanted to be able to lighten things up, but my mom and coach never allowed it. And so it was a sport I enjoyed that I never enjoyed.

No one here knows that I've never had a job before, that even at home I don't have chores. No one knows my dad is in court for real estate fraud. No one knows a thing. I've managed to get my work done and I'm feeling an approval from Pablo and Ren, like I'm not some spoiled white girl.

Nat walks through the swinging doors, making the sound I've come to enjoy. They're like doors in a saloon—you hear the creak and you look up, wondering who's going to come through.

He raises his eyebrows at me and walks toward the door that leads to the outdoor parking lot.

"Smoke break?" he asks.

I don't smoke.

"Sure," I say, and for some reason look over at Brose, who is openmouthed, head back, laughing at something Freddie is talking about. I'm caught off guard seeing him smile.

Nat lights up a joint, and while he takes a drag, he appraises me in a way that makes me both uncomfortable and highly flattered.

"What?" I say.

"Nothing." He laughs.

He passes the joint. I take a little drag and pass it back. "I thought you meant cigarette," I say, and smile in a way I hope is cute.

"Hell no," he says. "My grandpa died because of cigarettes."

The air is cold and clear. "I'm sorry," I say. "How old was he?"

"Ninety-two," he says, and I refrain from saying, *Maybe he died from being ninety-two.*

He hands me the joint again.

"All set," I say, holding up my hands. "I'm not super good at it."

"What are you good at?" He squints his eyes and takes a step back as if framing me for a shot.

I try to think of something. I shop well. I watch TV well. I skate well, but I don't want that to be part of my new persona. At summer camp I was surprisingly good at archery.

"Um," I say. "Shooting." I don't want to say "archery" and sound like one of those Renaissance fair weirdos.

"Shooting? Like, guns?" he says, clearly freaked out.

I need to rescue myself. Gun fanatics are a hundred percent worse than Renaissance fanatics. At least the Renaissance people seem educated.

"No, like . . . photography," I say. "Mountains and lakes,

uh . . . I'm trying to create a moving record of Colorado's transformation."

"Oh, wow," he says, and looks serious, but I can tell he's just being polite. This is much too artsy for him.

"Hey, you should come out with us." He puts the joint on the ground and squishes it with his shoe.

"Yeah," I say. "Okay."

I rub my hands up and down my arms. He puts his hand on my back as we walk toward the door. "You chilly?" he says, and I laugh, even though it wasn't funny.

When I'm finally done with the dishes, I walk out of the kitchen to the bar area, which is packed. Skip is behind the bar helping Jessica, the super-sweet bartender, who is all smiles and boobs.

"How's it going?" Skip says.

"Good," I say, kind of shy to admit how good it is. Skip was right. I haven't thought about my dad or Cee and her stupid texts. Rickie comes out of the kitchen and pats my head. She's about two heads taller than me.

"Can I go out with everyone? They're going to Eric's for pizza."

Skip pours a beer into a frosty glass. "Sure," he says. He looks at me with pride. It's like he stops what he's doing and just soaks in the moment. "Be good," he says.

"What else is there to be?" Rickie says. She hooks her elbow into mine and pulls. This is what I want.

Rickie and I sit at a table in back, away from the sounds of the arcade games where the boys have gone. In back of us is a booth full of guys loudly cheering at some game on TV. At the table next to us is a family, and I keep looking over at them, feeling both dismissive and envious.

"So how long are you staying with Skip?" Rickie asks, across the table from me. She has a fry in her mouth that she's biting but not eating, like it's a stick or a cigar.

"Just for winter break," I say. I fiddle with the salt and pepper.

"And then you go back to . . ."

"Colorado Springs," I lie.

"Ah," she says.

"And you live here, right?"

"I do," she says. "I'm a senior. You?"

"Sophomore." I can see her being a senior. I can just as easily picture her as a college grad, living on her own. She seems so much older than me.

"Cool. And why are you staying with Skip? Just for fun?"

"My parents are getting a divorce," I say, which doesn't sound like a lie once I say it. It feels inevitable somehow, and the thought makes me anxious. Was my mom prepared for this? Does she feel betrayed? If my dad loses, will she be there for him? My eyes water and blink quickly.

"Sorry," she says.

"It's fine," I say. "It's for the best." I take a long drink from my Sprite to buy some time. "My dad . . . he cheated, and it's the talk of the town."

"Oh, wow," she says, squirting mayonnaise into the bowl of ketchup, then stirring it with a fry. "How's that going?"

I roll my eyes. "It sucks. It was totally unexpected. We never imagined he could do something like it. And now our family . . . is like a freak show. Like everyone's looking at us, judging us, even though we didn't do anything wrong. And he may not have either. My mom just *thinks* he cheated."

I realize I've raised my voice and I'm drowning a fry in the mayo-ketchup concoction.

Rickie puts her hand on my arm.

"Sorry," I say. "Got carried away." And I did. I guess I'm not used to being so honest, even though I'm not being honest at all.

"It's good you're here, then," Rickie says. "You can hide out for a bit."

"That's the plan," I say.

She looks toward the front, and I see Brose and Forest and then Nat and Cara, following behind. They sit down, and Forest continues with the story he was already telling them, and the table's atmosphere changes completely. When we first planned on coming out, I envisioned sitting here with Nat. Now I look across the table at Rickie and wish it was just us. We could keep talking, telling both truth and lies.

Brose is talking to Cara. Everyone is laughing at whatever Forest is saying. I feel dismissed, not into it, wanting to go back to reality with Rickie, even though it wasn't reality at all. But it was steps toward it.

Nat smiles at me from across the table, and I perk up a bit, but never quite get into a groove.

When I get home, I call my dad, but of course he doesn't answer.

Did you cheat people? I want to ask. *Or are you just being wrongfully accused?*

Then a question for myself: *If he did cheat, would you want him to get away with it?*

Yes, I think, imagining the consequences—the shame, the erasing of everything we have. *I would.*

11

It's New Year's Eve and only my third day working here. I've always hated the event of New Year's, the pressure to have plans, so while I'm glad to be working, I'm nervous. Not nervous exactly—yesterday went pretty well—but I'm filled with even more adrenaline than usual. I expect it to be frantic, crazy, but when I said to Ren, "Tonight's going to be a madhouse," liking the way I felt like an insider when I said it, Brose informed me (mumbled, scoffed) that it's actually easier, since food service stops at ten.

"And no one cares what it tastes like," he said.

I rolled my eyes to myself, but as the night goes on, I see that he's right. It's busy, but fun. The cooks are relaxed, goofy, and a lot of the waiters have left earlier than usual since all the activity is at the bar.

The waitstaff wear New Year's flair—tinsel and glittery headbands in their hair. Every time the doors swing open, I look over, hoping to see Nat, that he hasn't left early. When it's him, I get this fluttering in my body, a brief possession. He always looks at me when he comes in, communicating something with his smirk, his eyes. I'd like to know exactly what he's trying to say. This time, he doesn't look at me. Layla and Tamara follow him in, and they're all chatting. They wait at the counter for their orders and the girls laugh at something Nat has said, but it's a cruel kind of laughter, an evil quack. When Layla catches me looking at them, I unclench my jaw and she gives me a very fake smile—she may as well have stuck her tongue out at me. I would have respected that.

"Hey, dishwasher," Nat says.

I hold down a grin. "Hey."

"You got plans tonight?"

"Not really," I say.

"Everyone who gets off at ten is heading to this party."

"Caps are up," Freddie calls.

Nat takes the plate of mushrooms, then says something to Layla, making her cackle.

"You should come," Brose says after Nat leaves, and I look up at him, surprised he'd have the same plans as them.

"Sure," I say. "Sounds like a hog-killin' time."

"A what?" Brose laughs, kind of through his nose, and I smile, because that was a real laugh.

"Hog-killin' time," I say. "Like, super fun. It's a little Western slang."

He nose-laughs again and goes back to dicing onions. "Rad," he says. "That's slang for radical." And I laugh, too.

I have to yell to Skip since it's so loud at the bar. It's a mixture of young and old people all standing close together. I've never wanted to spend New Year's this way: squished and yelling like you're at a concert but without a band.

"Can I go to a party with everyone?" I ask.

"Sure!" he says. "Be home after you bring in the new year, okay?" He looks at Rickie. "Get her home."

"Yes, boss," she says.

Jessica reaches for a bottle of vodka, and Skip gets hit by a boob.

"Excuse me," he says to Jessica, even though she didn't even notice—those things probably have a life of their own. I follow Rickie through the crowd to the front door. When we get outside, the raw air is like a gift.

I sit next to Nat in the back seat of Rickie's car. We're sharing his beer, which I pretend is normal and nothing special, though I usually don't drink. His arm is pressed against the side of my body, but it has to be because we packed four in the back. I'm against the window. I like the excuse to be so close.

"Who are you?" Tamara says from the front seat, turning to look at me. She's seen me countless times in the kitchen. It's funny—this reverse snobbery. These girls with tattoos and scrubby clothes being just as judgmental as the girls I know with high ponytails and Kate Spade clothes.

"I'm Annie," I say.

"Why are you here?" she asks.

"Jesus, Tam, you're such a bee-atch," Rickie says, and laughs.

What a weird and lame question. I try to say that I'm here to go to the party just like she is, but I mess up, dropping a few words and say instead, "I'm here to party."

Everyone laughs except for her. Brose, who is against the

other window, smiles into his fist, then says, "She's here to have a hog-killin' time," and I smile hard, but stop when I notice that he isn't. He's just looking out the window, not making an inside joke, just making fun of me. Who cares. I look down at Nat's leg pressing into mine. Here I am with the preppy boy. Though I tried to be Annie Town, I guess I'll stick to my own kind. Tamara turns the music up, and we go past the town, then onto a lightless road that smells of pine trees and campfires.

"Did you survive tonight?" Nat says, his breath on my forehead.

"I made it," I say.

"If you survived tonight, you could pretty much do anything," he says.

"Seemed like a pretty easygoing night to me," Brose says.

"Yeah, I guess," Nat says, and rolls his eyes at me, like the kitchen people are third-class citizens, or maybe the eye roll was meant to imply that Brose is an uptight dork. I return the eye roll, wanting to please the front of the house. I take a sip of his beer, then bring it down on his leg.

Rickie turns off the dark highway and onto a dirt road hedged on both sides with snow. She goes slow, and we bounce around over potholes. We round a bend, and there's a house lit up ahead. She parks by an empty skate ramp.

"Okay, kids," Rickie says. "We are here to party."

The house must have been rented by kids, because I can't imagine adults living here. There's hardly any furniture, and the windowsills are lined with empty liquor bottles. I wonder if mostly everyone is out of high school here or if, since this is a resort town, it's normal for high school kids to go to parties like this.

I trail Rickie for a while, smiling at her jokes, trying to contribute when we're with a group. When she heads off somewhere, I wander around pretending to look for the keg or the bathroom and end up going to the keg and the bathroom a lot. I'm not sure where Nat has gone, and I wish I could find him so I don't feel so awkward. On my next round to the keg, Brose is there, sitting on the kitchen counter looking content and peaceful. It's sort of like the look he has in the kitchen as the night progresses. I notice he starts out with a furrowed brow that eventually irons out.

"Hey there, Annie," he says, and I don't like the sound of my name in his mouth. He makes it sound so precious.

"Hey, Brose," I say, trying to make his name sound just as lame. "Having fun?"

"Yeah," he says, then shrugs. "But sometimes the best part about parties is the coming and going."

I know what he means, thinking about the car ride, how it in itself was like a celebration, but I don't respond.

He slides off the counter and takes my cup, tilts it into the hose. "Any New Year's resolutions?" He hands me my cup.

"Um . . ." I take a sip, then lick the foam off my lip. "Have more fun?" It sounds trivial, but maybe it's a worthy goal. For as long as I can remember, my life has revolved around skating, all my focus on training and not falling behind in school, on *not* letting myself have fun. Having this as a goal feels worthy. It's been like a secret to me—not being shaken to the core about not skating anymore. It's like getting dumped by someone you're obsessed with, only to realize you're so much healthier without them.

"Mine's to have less," Brose says. He's very thin and tall, yet when you get a closer look, he's substantial—like there's a lot going on under those clothes.

"Why less?" I ask, somewhat pleased he seems to be warming up to me.

"Oh, some of us have to work. Make money for college, figure out what we want to do with our lives, you know, the basics."

I *don't* know. It has never crossed my mind until now, really, to make money for college. Of course I think sometimes—but never too hard—about what I might do. I've always assumed I'd work for my father. But now what's going to happen? What if he has no business to run? What if we have no money?

"Some of us?" I ask.

He looks at my hair, my outfit—so basic, he doesn't even know—then back to my face.

"Quick quiz," he says. "Be honest. Is this job temporary?" he asks.

"Yes," I say.

"Will you work when school starts?"

"Um, no, I don't—"

"Private school?"

"Yes." I take a sip.

"What do your parents do?"

"None of your business," I say.

"Some of us," he says, then takes a sip as if it's a celebratory lap.

I could have lied about it all, but his rapid-fire round pinned me.

"And why would any of those things stop me from wanting to work hard, to have goals?"

"I didn't say anything about wanting to," he says. "I'm talking about *needing* to." He takes a sip, but keeps eye contact. "Why do you want to have more fun?"

I look around at the revelers, all making faces like they're wasted or shocked to hear something.

Something about Brose makes it hard to lie, to pretend I'm someone else. If anything, his aggression makes me want to expose and defend myself. I lean against the counter, slowing my heartbeat. "Because I haven't really had any before," I say, which comes off as sort of sad. I look around for other company. He's such a downer. "But cheers to you figuring it out. Us spoiled private school girls will never have to." I tap his cup, which makes a bit of beer spill out on his shoe. "Sorry," I say. "I'll buy you some new ones. Easy."

Rickie comes up to us. "Yo," she says. She pumps the keg, then takes the hose. "What's up?" She registers our hostility, but interprets it as disappointment with the party. "No good?" She looks around the room. "Yea or nay?"

"May as well hang out," Brose says, taking his phone out of his pocket. "Forty minutes until midnight."

"Oh my god," Rickie says. "Natty is totally fucking you right now."

I look down at my leg for some reason, then around the room.

"Don't look," she says, "or look, whatever."

He's across the room, talking to a few girls, but looking over at us, or me.

"He's fucking you with his eyes," Rickie says.

"What are you talking about?" I smile, but I'm looking at Nat, so he smiles back.

"Oops, he just came," Rickie says.

"That would be my cue," Brose says, walking past me. "Have fun." He holds up his cup, and I hold mine up, too.

"Have less," I say.

An old Britney Spears song comes on, and Rickie and I start to dance, and I laugh a bit too loudly, pretending I'm just here in the moment, even though I'm highly aware of Nat's gaze, not knowing if it's on me or not, but acting like it is. Every move from head to tail is for him. Nothing wasted. It's New Year's Eve, and I want to have so much fun behaving like the kind of girl I never thought I wanted to be. Rickie and I dance out of the kitchen toward the group of dancers in the living room. Beer sloshes on the carpet and on people's shoes, but no one cares. We're all so young, and we know it. Clap your hands.

I rest against the railing outside, then lean back while holding on like I'm water-skiing. Someone grabs me by the waist, and for a moment I don't turn, giving in to the mystery. It could only be one person, and I came out here specifically so that one person could catch me alone. The mystery pushes me back to the rail and clasps his hands around me. I turn my head, and there's Nat. I feel warm where he's touched me. I feel warm everywhere. He lets go and stands next to me.

"I thought I should hug you before we kiss at midnight," he says.

"Oh, is that what we're doing?" I keep looking ahead.

"Well, you can't kiss yourself," he says. "I thought I'd do you a favor."

I shake my head. "Oh my god," I say, pretending to be incredulous. I walk down the steps.

"Come on," he says, following me. "We have ten minutes. And I'm just kidding. We can hug at midnight, or talk, or do snow angels. Whatever."

"I'll kiss you," I say, feeling bold in the dark woods. I lean back against a tree, hoping I look sexy like Sadie always manages to do, even when she's just standing still. He stands in front of me, looking at me lazily; his face is slack. He sways a bit, and I think I may be swaying too.

"Should we practice?" he asks. He twists his mouth, then covers it with his hand. I like the way his jeans fit, the way he smells like smoke, and before I know it, I'm moving toward him and then his hand is behind my head and we're kissing. Slowly, deeply, and my head spins a bit. I grab him around the waist to hold on. We continue to kiss, and it's like we're desperate for it, like we're taking in something essential. It all feels set to music, arranged by experts. This is how people fall in love.

But I'm not falling in love—my mind is too busy, thinking ahead, planning what to do, what not to do, wondering if I'm doing anything right. He presses himself against me, and I press back, and in the distance I hear voices, people counting: ten, nine, eight . . . I move my hands under his shirt to feel the skin on his back, and he shivers a bit, then does the same to me, except up the front of my shirt, his hand under my bra.

"God, your body," he says.

Well fueled and sculpted, I know, and not in a conceited way. Skating will do that to you.

I don't know what road I'm on, whose house I'm at. My parents are so far in the distance somewhere. I can't imagine their voices. How did I get here, doing what I'm doing? It's so unexpected, such a thrill to get off track and be lost. For a second I open my eyes to see where I am: trees pointing toward infinity and a spray of vivid stars. I think of Sadie again, what she said to my brother when we were leaving the house, something like: "I'd go down on you if your sister wasn't here," and I think, *This isn't me standing here, anyway*. This is Annie Town, some other girl in some other place. A wild girl, a free girl, a crazy, cool girl. A girl Brose has no right to judge. *Stop thinking about Brose,* I think to myself. *He's no fun. And he has a stupid name.*

"Happy New Year's," Nat says, and I come back to him. I hear everyone in the distance cheering, and the sound of fireworks.

"Very happy," I say, and we kiss again, and then, for the first time ever, because I want to, because I can—I make my way down.

12

I leave with Rickie at around one. I'm glad everyone else got their own rides and it's just us. We're both too tired to talk, and I'm relieved. There's a slow song on the radio, and it's making everything that just happened seem more distant and abstract. The guitar, strings, and vocals are a soundtrack to a random montage. I'm a character in a—

"Did you hook up with Nat?" Rickie asks.

The scene I was creating blackens. I look ahead at the swath of road lit in the headlights, making it seem like we're going into a tunnel.

"Kind of," I say.

"Kind of," she says, and smirks.

"You?" I ask, to take the attention away. "Kiss anyone at midnight?" I roll my eyes at myself.

"I kissed Tam at midnight, but . . . nothing new there."

Rickie looks over at me, gauging my response. I try to keep my expression unreadable, but I'm surprised, I guess, and feel kind of shy and naive. Does she mean kissing Tamara is nothing new and that she's gay, or did she just randomly kiss a girl as girls sometimes do, usually in front of others? Max and Brodhi—two senior guys at my school—are clearly gay and out about it, but there are no out girls that I know of. Especially no one like Rickie. I stare at her full lips, imagining them kissing Tamara.

"She was jealous," she says.

"Of what?" I ask.

Rickie tilts her head toward me.

"Me?"

"She gets jealous of every girl I hang out with. And then I had to take you home."

"I'm sorry," I say.

"No, I wanted to go home," she says. "I'm a home girl. She can stay out till breakfast."

"She has nothing to be jealous of," I say.

"I know," Rickie says, and even though she's just confirming what I said, it stings a little.

She stops in front of the house, the Santa on the Harley like a beacon. Seeing it makes me sad all of a sudden, nostalgic for a childhood I never really had, one with silly and vulgar toys. I put a stick of gum in my mouth, and when I get out of the car, the mint and the cold feel like a breeze in my face.

"Nighty night," Rickie says through a yawn.

"Happy New Year," I say.

"Happy New Year," she says, and blows me a kiss. "Fresh start."

"I hope so," I say.

I open the front door slowly to a dark room with a soft glow of auburn light. I don't want to see Jay right now. I feel like a different sister, a disappointing, slutty one. A weaker one.

I hear a cough and freeze, but then I don't hear anything, so I close the door behind me and look around the empty room. I take off my coat and hear more coughing and see smoke rising from the kitchen counter and then Nicole stands up, revealing herself and the joint in her hand.

"Hey," she says, then coughs some more, but with a closed mouth. "I'm screwed," she says. "Too much . . . I'm sorry you had to see this. Pot is bad . . . very, very bad. But you don't cough, you don't get off."

I've smoked weed with Jay and thought it was okay. It made watching movies kind of fun—but I couldn't focus on the stories. My mind would keep opening new doors. Because of these weird circumstances and because I feel alive but sad and icky, I walk over to her and reach for the joint.

She backs up. "Oh no, you don't."

"Come on," I say. "I've had a bad night and a good night."

"I don't care," she says. "You're . . . a young person."

"It's legal," I say.

"For me," she says, but a smile is kind of breaking through her face. I try again, and she holds it up, but I jump and get it because I'm a cat. I inhale. She watches me, flabbergasted.

"Shit, you really wanted that," she says.

I smile, cough once.

"Why was your night bad?" she asks. She hops up to sit on the counter, and I do the same.

"It wasn't bad bad," I say, thinking about it. "I just wasn't myself, and it . . . left me with a bad taste in my mouth." I stop chewing my gum and try to look at her out of the corner of my eye. That was just foul. "Aren't you trying to get pregnant?" I ask. "What if you're pregnant right now?"

"God, you sound just like Skip," she says. "We've been trying for, like, ten years. So what, I just stop living my life? I sacrifice my hobbies?"

"Smoking weed is your hobby?"

"No," she says, and sounds like a teenager. "But it seriously can't be worse than the drugs you have to take to get you fertile. I mean, that makes you shit-bat crazy. I take breaks from them so I don't bash Skip's head in." She smiles a little, maybe testing. "Sorry. Too much information. TMI."

"You don't need to abbreviate," I say. "I actually like to say all the words. Oh my god."

We are quiet for a while, both kicking the counter. I can't believe I just smoked with my aunt.

"Isn't it batshit crazy?" I ask. "Not shit-bat." I smile to myself at the way it sounds.

"I like to mix things up."

"I guess I'll go to bed," I say.

"This will not happen again, okay?" she says, searching my face. "You will never tell your mom about this ever. And we will not chill like homies. This isn't a thing."

I smile, and she concentrates on keeping a straight face. "Your loss," I say, and she holds back a laugh like it's a cough.

"From now on, when you're here, I'm your . . . I'm your mom," she says.

You're nothing like my mom, I almost say, but she's not saying she is, and saying it aloud would sound like an insult. She's nothing like my mom in that my mom wouldn't see me coming in late. Our house is too big. My mom would never smoke pot. She's always in control. Even her Chardonnay buzz seems like something she's putting on. My mom isn't funny or weird. I love her, but she's like this beautiful thing with an impenetrable surface, like there's an unripe skin on her. Then I realize that people probably think the exact same thing about me. That I'm impenetrable. Unreal.

"Where's Jay?" Nicole asks.

"No clue," I say. "Maybe back in Genesee, or his boys all came to him."

"I know it's New Year's Eve, but you kids need to realize that—that we're, like, the adults."

I look her over. She doesn't look like an adult and seems unconvinced of the role. The extinguished joint is on the counter. She sees me looking at it.

"Let's say we get a hall pass tonight." She touches her stomach, something I've noticed her doing a lot, like a nervous twitch. I like the idea of the hall pass. We're all excused and can resume tomorrow, free and clear. That's kind of what staying with them has been like. We can do things we regret, things out of character, then reemerge free and clear. Except this won't last once we return to our real lives.

"Want to watch a little TV?" she asks.

"Okay."

We sit on opposite corners of the couch, watching a reality show about people addicted to plastic surgery. It's like watching a show about walking carp. Sometimes we laugh at the same time, which is cool and awkward. I don't know what I'm paying attention to more: the show or her sitting next to me. I'm aware of my breath and every time I shift on the couch.

"These people are idiots," she says. "But what does that make us?"

"Truth seekers," I say, and she kind of smiles, as if unsure how to read this weirdo that is me.

"Want to watch a Western?" I ask.

"Sure," she says.

I go to the room and grab *A Fistful of Dollars*, a Clint Eastwood movie about a wandering gunfighter messing with the heads of two rival families. I love the hats in this one and the way he rocks the blanket poncho. I have one just like it that I wear with my brown boots.

We watch for a long time, and I'm kind of impressed with her stamina and relieved by it, too. Nothing's worse than sharing something with someone and having them return it without even trying it on.

"I can't put you together," she says at one point, and I don't bother to answer. In a way, it's the nicest thing anyone's ever said to me. It makes me happy.

When I see she's asleep, I turn the TV off and go back to my room. I wonder what Nat is thinking. We left off walking back to the party. We held hands until we reached the top of the porch steps and then he let go. I've tried not to overthink it—the way he never talked to me afterward. It was my choice, after all.

13

Nat was off yesterday. I was disappointed, but then kind of relieved. I don't know why I did what I did, but I'm glad I got it over with, I guess. At least now I know what to do. He's supposed to be working today and could walk in at any moment, so I've been aware of myself like I'm onstage.

"Last one," Ren says, talking about the shrimp. "You are fast," he says.

"What should I do now?" I wipe my hands on my apron.

He nods toward Brose. "You can help him."

Great. I walk over to his counter to see if he has a chore for me. "Can I do anything?" I ask.

He's massaging a hamburger patty, pressing the edges into little walls.

"You look like you really care about that patty," I say.

"I do," he says. "Getting it ready to go out into the world."

He takes his glove off, then dips a carrot into a white, creamy sauce, takes a bite, and looks at me like he can't figure it out.

"Taste," he says, holding the dipped carrot in front of my face.

I hesitate, then bite. It's tangy and garlicky, delicious. "Needs more salt."

"You always say that," he says.

Agreed. Yesterday when he fed me a bite of buffalo, I said it, and with the mushrooms I said it, too. "It's always the answer." I hold his gaze. "It brings out the best of what's already there." I feel shy all of a sudden. "Anyway, can I help?"

"Do you really want to? Get your hands dirty?"

"Gloves," I say. I put on a pair, snapping one when I'm done.

"You can help," he says. "But you have to take my direction. I'm a patty perfectionist."

"I'm kind of a perfectionist myself."

He looks me up and down, and I'm aware of my hair in a low bun, my clean Marc Jacobs booties, totally kitchen inappropriate. I wore jeans, at least.

"I gathered that," he says, then looks down at his work.

"And I know how to make patties," I say.

"But do you?" he asks. "It's all in the thumbs. Actually, there's more to it than that. If you really want to know how to make the best hamburgers, it involves more than thumbs."

I'm about to ask what else is involved because it's interesting and not my specialty, but then I hear "You guys miss me?" and Nat walks in through the swinging doors. I straighten up, look down at my awful plastic apron, my kitchen-gloved hands submersed in raw meat.

Pablo and Ren exchange looks at Nat's bluster. I think I detected some eye rolling.

"What's up, dishwasher?" he says.

I don't answer, because he's moved on, greeting everyone, though no one seems to greet him back as heartily. I have a feeling no one back here really likes Nat. He's like me, I realize, though no one here knows the exact extent of this—he's clean-cut, temporary, having—but not needing—a job. After asking Freddie about the specials—caribou and trout—he turns to go, but before he leaves, I say, "Hey, Natty?"

"Yo," he says, looking up from his phone, impatiently, like I'm bothering him, like he's never kissed me before. I know guys can be assholes. I'm not some babe in the woods, but just logically, I did something pretty cool with him, for him, and as a guy, wouldn't he want me to do that cool something again? Not that I would or want to really, but still. It's in his best interest to be kind.

"Want to go outside?" I ask, gesturing that we could smoke, which makes me feel like an uncool person imitating a cool one.

"Um, okay?" he says, not making eye contact. "Give me ten. I'll meet you out there."

He goes back to the dining room. I take off my smock of shame.

"Give him ten," Brose says, with his deep voice that sounds nothing like Nat's, but I don't answer or look at him because, for some reason, I respect Brose. I'd like his approval, and I know I won't find it in his eyes right now.

When I go outside, Nat's there with Rickie and Layla. Rickie looks annoyed. Layla looks like she's in love. She bumps her head into Nat's shoulder like a kitten. I feel like a dumb ass. And yet, Rickie's here, and I am buoyed by her.

"What's up, dishwasher?" Nat says again. "You wanted me to come out and smoke, so smoke." He exchanges looks with Layla, communicating, at least in my eyes, that I'm pathetic. Insignificant. He's outing me in front of this girl and Rickie—

telling them I wanted to be out here with him but the feeling isn't mutual.

"I just . . . wanted to say hey," I say.

Rickie raises her eyebrows and looks back and forth between the two of us.

Nat turns to Layla and they talk about something, but I don't hear it. I want to leave, but don't know how.

"Dude," Rickie says. "Didn't you guys just hook up?"

I can't believe she said that, and yet I'm somewhat grateful. He stops talking and looks at me, then away.

"No," he says, his eyes on Layla.

I feel like I'm in a trance. I can't focus on anything. Is this what happens? How was he so nice, so into me, and now it's like I'm some kind of rash?

"I gave him a blow job," I say. I actually say this out loud, and for some reason, my words carry the tint of a British accent. Oh my god. It's like I just woke up from a coma and blurted out the first thing that came to my mind.

Rickie looks at me, both appalled and thrilled, her mouth in a big O.

"Oh my god." Layla laughs-not-really-laughs. "Um," she says. "Okay?" Punctuating her stupid laugh with a stupid affectation. I want to pour the bucket of shrimp tails over her head and be all, *Um. Okay? Ha ha?*

She communicates to Nat with her eyes: *What a psycho.* I try my best to communicate to her: *I'm going to shrimp-tail your ass, bitch.* But wait. I look at Nat—he's my focus, not her. She did nothing. He's making us do all the work, taking the focus off of him.

He smiles, looks down, then shakes his head. "I'm outta here."

"Um, yeah," Layla says.

She walks toward the kitchen door, but he walks to the front of the restaurant, not checking to see if she's following. She opens the door, then sees him walking the other way, hesitates, and runs to catch up with him.

I kick the potholed-parking-lot snow dirt. I have never experienced anything like this before—pure humiliation mixed with rage, mixed with a little bit of conviction—like, I'm working with logic here, and that dude was not working with me! Is this what boys are like? Does everyone know this already?

"Holy shit," Rickie says, putting her hand on my back. "You sort of owned that moment in a really weird way."

"I went with my instincts," I mumble. The air is punishing, the mountain glaringly white. Rickie winds the scarf tighter around my neck. It feels motherly and nice.

"Nat's not the best guy," she says. She pulls my beanie down to cover my ears. "Layla's not even his girlfriend. His girlfriend works at the brewery. She's Swedish. I mean, not really, but one of those girls who looks Swedish. All clean and blond and shit."

Like me, I think, but undisguised. "I feel so stupid."

She nods, not bothering to object. "Did you sleep with him?" she asks.

I blink. "No. I've never even . . . done that before. I just . . . sucked him off."

"Jesus! Why'd you say it that way?"

"I don't know. It just came out. Everything's just coming out. My instincts have always been off." I shift from foot to foot. "God, gross, I feel really gross. I'd never done *that* before either."

111

I look at her in a way that's pleading. I'm begging her to fix this. My first week here, and I'm already the slut in town. This almost makes me laugh. Who would have thought? At least I only have a week left. Remembering this time line kind of shocks me—how fast the days have gone by, how at times I forget about the upcoming verdict. I never expected to think about anything else, really.

"It'll be okay," Rickie says, and seems to really consider this.

"They're going to go back in there and blab my moment."

She nods again. Like a judge. "Yeah," she says. "Probably."

"What should I do?"

We move out of the way for a car. There's an old lady driver gripping the steering wheel and leaning forward to see. I wonder if she's done anything slutty in her life. I kind of laugh thinking about it, and then imagine myself old and some kid laughing about me getting it on and feel defensive, like *I did it. We all do it. That's why we're here!*

"I don't think you need to do anything," she says. "You already did it. Some advice, though? Don't do that again. Guys get all weird and entitled. Oh my god, don't cry."

I'm not crying, just on the verge. I don't know how I can be both so abrasive and so soft. I'm like a sponge with a scouring pad.

She touches my shoulders. "It's going to be okay. Move on, forget about him. Be you."

"Okay," I say, and sniffle.

"Though I have no idea who you are," she says.

"Me neither," I say, which makes me tear up. Who am I when I'm home, with my adult shoes, my self-restrictions and rules, this longing to grow up and be like a man who may be full of deception and greed? Who am I here, trying to be someone else, which is so planned and fake?

Rickie holds my shoulders. Her eyes big and dark. "No bj's," she says.

"Okay," I say, grinning slightly.

"You get why?"

I look into her kind eyes. She may not know who I am, but she sees me. "I get it, yeah."

"I mean, unless you want to, but it should be reciprocated . . . if you want it to be."

"Are those your rules?" I ask.

"I guess," she says. "For now, at least. Rules are always changing."

"Right," I say, thinking I understand.

"Did you even like him?" she asks.

I kick the gravel again. "I mean, I thought he was cute. I like him. I liked him." I take a moment to think about what I'm trying to say. "Yeah, I liked him, and I . . . I just wanted to try it?"

"I get it," she says, and I believe she does.

"But now what?" I ask. "Is it just done with us?"

"It sure seems like it," she says, moving her hands off my shoulders. "You want to know the truth?"

I nod.

"He'll assume you'll get with him again. He'll count on it. If I were you, I wouldn't let him touch you." She shakes my wrist.

"Good advice," I say.

14

Day three of the new year, and I wake up to the smell of bacon, but then I realize I fell asleep in the clothes I wore last night and it's not fresh bacon. It's the old scent of bacon-wrapped shrimp, clinging to my sweatshirt. I didn't brush my teeth either, or floss—there goes a year of my life, pretty much. I didn't wash my face, something I never forget to do. Exfoliate, tone, hydrate.

After work I went out with Rickie to some bar where she knows the bartender so we wouldn't get carded. Brose came, too, and I vaguely remember dancing near him on a floor that was covered with peanut shells. I don't know what depresses me more—the fact that I feel like bunk or that people eat peanuts and throw the shells on the floor. What's the point? It gives me a small taste of what we all would do if we were allowed to do it. We're savages—all of us. I get out of bed and kick and punch the air, tricking my body into enthusiasm for the day.

I walk out to the hall and hear the voices of Skip and Nicole, and I stop to snoop, since I hear my name. I peek around the wall to see Nicole's butt in the air, a downward dog. I move back to hiding and am startled by a picture of my mom, my young mom next to a young Nicole, who's holding a bouquet on what is obviously her wedding day.

"It's fine," Skip says. "She's been happy all week. She's like the young Buddha, seeing what's on the other side of the castle wall."

I puff out my cheeks, Buddha-like. I have no idea what he's talking about.

"She's not exactly Buddha, honey," Nicole says, short of breath. "He didn't get to the other side and buy a flat-screen and a new wardrobe."

Are they arguing about me buying things for my room? Why would they care?

"She's just trying to make it her home. And the clothes—I mean, she came here looking like a socialite or something, and now she's . . . She fits in with the kids."

"Grunge-chic," Nicole says. "Just like Buddha. Free People. Two hundred bucks for a slashed sweater. Enlightened."

"I don't know what that means," Skip says, and I look down at my clothes—bell-bottom jeans and a damn Free People blouse. I go to my room, throw on a sweater before coming back out. I peek around again. Nicole is doing some crazy stretching and yoga moves, which Skip seems to find arousing. His head is tilted.

"It's not right," she says. "Spending money at a time like this—did you see the news this morning? That lady lost her entire pension! Entire! Poof!"

"She doesn't know—"

I press my back against the wall, wondering who the lady was that lost her pension, and also wanting to know when my dad will return my calls to explain. I look at the pictures of Skip and Nicole. They were so cute and young together. God, they have so many pictures of themselves. They did selfies before there was even a name for it. They were pioneers. And there's Jay's school photo that I keep landing on. His kindergarten one, perhaps—his two front teeth missing.

"The late hours," I hear Nicole say. "She got home at one in the morning! You've put her in this horrible environment."

"My restaurant?"

"Yes! We met at the restaurant, remember? The drinking, the drugs, we had sex in the walk-in fridge!"

Oh my god. I hold my breath.

"That was great," Skip says. "Our anniversary's coming up if you want a redo." I peek around the wall, and Nicole is glaring at him.

"Annie's fine," he says. "I'm watching her. I'm on it."

He is so not on it. I'm hungover and look like I've been hit with a sack of flour. I make my entrance, rubbing my eyes and fake yawning. They look like they've been caught doing it in a walk-in fridge.

"Hey," I say. They exchange looks. I go to the kitchen and pour myself a huge glass of juice and a bowl of cereal, then sit to watch TV. I can feel them behind me playing charades.

"We're going to hit the mountain," Skip says. I turn to look at him. I've been raised that way.

"Want to come with us?"

"I'm meeting Rickie," I say. "We're golfing."

"It's winter," Nicole says. She seems very annoyed with me.

"Virtual," I say.

They do the look exchange again, and I wait politely, chewing with my mouth closed.

Nicole crosses her arms in front of her chest, her lips in a strong pout.

"Hey, I know it's not our place," he says.

"Well," she says. "It is. It is our place." Her smile manages to be unfriendly.

"We want you to be comfortable living here, but we also want you to live here, in the home we have," Skip says.

I look around at the home that they have, the small brick fireplace, the black leather sofa, faded curtains, tan carpet. It reminds me of the condo development in Eagle that my dad bought and tore down.

"That other TV didn't work so well," I say. "I asked my mom. She said it was fine. It's on me."

I look down. Nicole's eyes are mean. "It's not *on you*. It's on your parents, and I don't need them buying us anything. Do you even understand what's happening?"

A tear slips, but I don't think they can see. I understand what's happening, but I just want my dad to do his thing—fight, win, and move on. What else is there to do about it? If he's right, he's right, and he needs to win and defend himself. The people who've lost—what can I do to help? What can he do?

"Thanks for thinking of us," Skip says. "But—"

"I don't see what the problem is," I say. "What's wrong with taking my parents' money? You're watching us. Babysitters make money."

Nicole gapes at me. Skip cringes like he was counting on me to say the right thing and I didn't come through.

"If I had a kid, and she spoke like that, I'd spank her," Nicole says. "I don't care what the policy is."

"Well, you don't have a kid," I say. "That ship has sailed."

Something holds her back from lunging at me. I saw the urge and then the restraint, and it both thrilled and terrified me. Her chest fills with air, her eye twitches. Skip puts his hand on her shoulder and squeezes, shaking his head at me. I catch a glimpse of something hateful in his eyes before it changes into disappointment, which feels worse. They both turn away from me, and I get up to finish breakfast in my room.

The truth is, I didn't speak to my mom about buying a TV or about anything. She never answers when I call, and when I texted, she just wrote back, **Do whatever.** It's how she's always been, but I thought during this time she'd become someone softer, someone I could depend on, someone who might even turn to me. I don't know why I was so rude to Nicole, why I said that about her kid or lack thereof. I don't know why I feel so junk after a fun night out. I don't know why I feel slapped by humiliation even though I brought it upon myself. It's like I'm in a dressing room and trying on these disguises, and none of them are flattering. I don't recognize myself anymore. I'm so cold I break my own heart.

15

I call my dad again but get no answer. I feel the way I do when Nat wouldn't talk to me—used and abandoned, dumb. My parents always thought I was too young to handle anything. Even though I'm not even two years younger than Jay, they trust him so much more. They don't even let me drive, and I'm not at all flattered by their protectiveness. I'd be more flattered by trust, by allowing me the same things as him.

I walk over to Jay's room. He's playing guitar in his ski pants, with no shirt on. What if I just walked around with no shirt?

"Have you talked to Mom and Dad since the other night?" I ask.

He strums. "Nope."

He focuses back on the guitar, playing a song I like. I groan, pretending I'm so tired of hearing this song, but then I decide to soften up. It's not like Jay's done anything wrong.

He slaps the strings. "You off to work?"

"Not till five." We both smile slightly, those truth smiles that don't come from a sarcastic place. They're rare and make something inside me whimper and flutter. We are communicating homesickness, I think. We are communicating how strange it is that we've only been here a little over a week and I have a job, that something interesting and different has come from our small disaster.

I look down at my phone to see if Cee has texted me back from earlier this morning. Nope. Big nopes from everyone. Her shunning me doesn't make any sense, despite the rift between our parents, and I'm getting tired of being the one to reach out. I have the right to be just as angry—her dad is betraying my dad by testifying. I should be the furious one. I guess the difference is she must know more, and I don't know enough to be really convinced of anything. She and her dad are close. He shares things with her. With me, too. At dinners he'd talk to us about work like we were his peers. He trusted our intelligence, and it makes me feel like a traitor that I can't summon the same anger Cee has, probably because I trust her dad, too.

"I wonder if Ken testified yet," I say.

"Yeah, I don't know," Jay says.

"Why don't we go talk to them?"

"Talk to the guy who's testifying against Dad?"

"It's Ken," I say. "We know him, and he's known us forever. He wouldn't just come out against Dad for no reason. I want to hear his side. Don't you?"

He looks down and strums, then slaps the body of the guitar, which means he's done. "He may not have a side. He may just be testifying—like, giving info, details. He may not even want to be doing it."

"That's why I want to go. Our own parents won't just lay it all out. He will. I know he'd tell me the truth. Will you take me?"

"Are you sure?" he asks, and he looks up. "I mean, you're sure you want it all laid out?"

Am I ready for the truth, he's asking, *no matter what it looks like?*

"I'm sure," I say.

No response. He looks around the room for something else to do.

"We can stop at Sadie's, too." I roll my eyes but hope it will seal the deal.

"She broke up with me," he says, and gets up, putting his guitar away.

"*She* broke up with *you*?"

"I know. Hard to believe." He smiles, but there's a tension around his mouth, a sadness in his eyes. "You know the deal. Her mom is friends with our mom, her dad, same circle, blah, blah, blah."

"We need to talk to Ken," I say.

He presses his thumb into his temple. I've never seen him look so tired. "All right," he says. "Let's go."

And so Sadie, in a way, still sealed the deal.

We head out of town to our town. I sit back, looking out the window at the lake, the mountains, these large and silent things that have been here forever.

Jay texted me an article to read while we drive, and I skim it over and feel like I'm reading something about someone I don't know.

"What's this Delaware stuff even about?" I ask, and his grip tightens on the steering wheel.

"I'm not completely sure," he says, oddly formal. "I guess we'll find out."

We go through the Eisenhower Tunnel. The other side is bright and sunny, and the simple and familiar black-and-white landscape—black rocks, white snow—fills me with affection.

"Do they know we're coming?" he asks.

"Yeah," I say. "I called Ken. He said we'd have a late lunch."

We head down, down, then through the narrow canyon. Rocks shed their snow, revealing their browns and reds. After the small tunnel, the homes on the mountain appear like castles. I never realized how fairy-tale-like our neighborhood is, guarded by a herd of buffalo, perched above the city like a kingdom. Jay is driving more carefully than usual. When we get closer to home, I sit up, almost nervous, like I don't belong here anymore.

"I can't believe we start school in a week," Jay says.

"I know, and we're still . . . not here. You think they'll be done with the trial and everything?"

"You'd think," he says. "And if not, I guess we'll be making this drive more often."

"Sucks," I say, and yet it doesn't seem so bad.

We turn into Cee's neighborhood, which is quiet and a lot different from our own, where houses are sometimes a ten-minute drive from one another.

Jay parks at the curb. I look at Cee's house, this staple in my life. It's funny that I was the one with the castle, and this was the home we preferred. We walk to the front door.

"I don't think I've ever gone through the front door," I say.

"Where do you usually go?" he asks.

"Garage," I say, but this seems like a front-door moment. I use the lion knocker, and soon after, Ken opens the door.

"Ah! Annie and the good brother." My instinct is to jump up and put my arms around him. How I love Ken Rush and his funny ways, but I just utter a weak hello.

"Come in," he says. "How nice of you to stop by." We walk in, and I just want to collapse on the slippery leather sofa and watch Netflix while Ken makes us variations of popcorn. Chile lime was one of my favorites.

"It truly grieves me that things have turned out this way," he says immediately, before I can take off my coat.

I look down, not knowing how to respond. He's not on our side. It's kind of awkward, to put it mildly.

"But, Annie," he says, "you and I—we want the same thing. For your friendship with Celia to remain intact."

"Thank you," I say, relieved he still wants me in their lives, that it's possible.

"And I'm pretty fond of both of you," he says, including Jay. "We all go way back." He smiles, contemplating something pleasant. "Now, I hope you don't mind, but I haven't told Celia you're coming. I didn't think she'd stick around."

"Oh," I say.

"Don't worry. We'll work things out. Ceci!" he calls. "Ceci. Look who's here."

I stop breathing, so nervous, as if I'm about to sing an aria. I stand close to Jay, and then there's Cee, her good ol' self, in her gray leggings and black sweatshirt. She hasn't grown since she was twelve. I just want to lift her up and spin her around. She pauses at the top of the staircase and shakes her head. I automatically raise my hand.

"Hi," I say, high-pitched, too thrilled to hold back. I should be defensive, nervous, but I can't help but go back to what it's always been. She quickly walks down the steps.

"C-Rush," Jay says. "What is up?"

I walk to meet her halfway, then notice that she isn't coming in for a greeting. Cee is about to fuck me up.

"Whoa," I say. "What the—"

"Celia!" her dad says, right as she tackles me to the ground.

"What is happening?" Jay says.

"What are you doing?" I yell. She's always had this temper, but she's acting like a two-year-old.

"You've fucked up my life," she says, pinning my arm over my head.

"Celia, we've talked about this," her dad says. "That is false. And this is not why we fight!"

Jay is trying to pry her off me, but Cee, being a state karate champ, swipes his legs out from under him. Jay lands awkwardly and bumps into a table.

"Ow!" he says. "My back!"

I try to roll her off, but she knees me in the side, then holds me under my arm.

"Celia, halt!" Ken says, and I start to laugh a little.

"That tickles," I say, a big mistake, because I get kneed again.

"Ow, come on!" I say.

Her face hovers above mine, her hair hitting my face.

"My dad's taking me and my sisters out of school," she says.

"I'm moving to my mom's in frickin' Kansas. Kansas! Your dad's a crook. He *stole* our money."

"So pin *him* to the ground!" I yell. "I'm sorry! Why do you think I'm here?"

Cee gives me a last shove, then stands.

"Why are you here?" she asks.

I catch my breath, rise up on my elbows. Everyone seems to be waiting for my answer. "Because I miss my friend," I say. "And I want you to talk to me."

Cee and I are on the couch. Jay is lying on his back with pillows propped under his knees. Ken is in his recliner, telling us, more or less, everything we want and don't want to hear. I catch Cee looking me over, wary, like she sees me as someone changed for the worse. She and her father are inextricable to me—my memories of her have traces of him, and I wonder if she links me in the same way to my dad. But of course she doesn't. He couldn't be in her memories. He never took us on hikes, or snowboarding, or picked us up from school. He never took us bowling or to his office. Ken even took us to see Twenty One Pilots in Park City for my fifteenth birthday. He later thanked us for exposing him to a "rather delightful band."

Ken makes sure I'm paying attention, then continues. "Your father was using everyone's deposits to pay an outside company registered in Delaware—consulting, architectural, engineering fees—"

"Which happens all the time," Jay says. I look down at

him on the floor. I'm always surprised by how much he knows. You'd think the popular guy in school wouldn't be the brightest, but nope.

Ken shakes his cocktail glass. "Yes, it does happen," Ken says, "but I believe, as do others, that this Delaware company is . . . well, not a company at all. It's his personal bank account."

Ken looks over his glass, as if measuring our capacity to hold all of this. I try not to blink. Jay's eyes are closed. A long blink. I do the same and let Ken's words move around me. Some ping off my skin, and some sink down to my core.

My father used people's money for himself. People's money and savings that they thought were going to a future home. According to Ken.

He continues. "As the majority owner of Tripp Land and Development, your dad has complete control over everything. He secures the financing, chooses the contractors, decides his bonus, et cetera, et alia."

I smile with my eyes closed. Ken always uses Latin words. I open my eyes, and he makes his footrest pop up.

"Everything he did was approved by two, quote, independent, end quote, directors on the board, but we think this was a rubber-stamp committee. They took excessive fees from your father—well, from our investments—to approve whatever he wanted. Are you following?"

"Yes," I say. Kind of. While I don't get all of the terms he uses, I do understand that what my dad has done is awful and deceitful. According to Ken.

Jay looks irritated, maybe because he understands. It wasn't supposed to unfold this way. I was prepared to hear things I didn't want to hear, but I guess I thought I could dismiss them more easily.

"But," I say. "He wouldn't intentionally take things from people." I don't dare look at Cee. I'm afraid she's smirking. "He worked all the time on this. He was so proud—"

"Of course he worked hard," Ken says, and takes a sip. "The problem is that when units weren't selling, his lifestyle—the one you've always had—didn't change, because he was hoping pre-sales would keep coming and that the general ledger line items would blend in. Following?"

I nod, thinking of our life, my coach and private skating time, the jet we take to Hawaii, or random football games in California or Seattle. Our maids, our chef, our parties, our clothes. What money was his to use and give away?

"I don't know what ledger line means," Jay says, "but I think I get it."

Unfortunately, I do too. If I'm going to take Ken's word, what he's saying is that my dad messed up, and when he knew he'd messed up, he didn't admit or fix it. He made it worse. My dad worked very hard, but when things went wrong, all he did was work hard at hiding it.

"Look," Ken says. "I'm no Leo the Great. For a long time the money was flowing like water—Blue Sky, Eagle, Ore Lofts—they did remarkably well. With this one in Denver, we expected even more, so I understand your dad got carried away, thinking he'd get it all back. I liked your father, but he was under a lot of pressure, and he got himself into a bear garden. These are criminal charges we're talking about, as you know, which will most likely be followed by civil charges. *Annus horribilis.*"

"You've got to stop saying that," Cee says, and when I look at her, we both can't help but smile, but just a little bit. A brief forgetting of where we are.

"But it's apt," Ken says.

"Do you have any proof?" Jay asks.

My stomach grumbles, and I push down on it.

"I have what I know," he says. "And at the trial I'm going to use it."

He must see my brief look of hostility. Part of me just can't believe it.

"I'm very sorry," Ken says. "But we're fighting. I'm fighting. These aren't just his rich friends or wealthy investors who took a little loss—these are hardworking families and employees who had hope and faith. And it's not just investors. There were contractors, builders like Desjarlais Construction, who never got paid. The owner had to cover the cost, fire his crew. Some people are in a very grave bind. All are belching smoke from the seven orifices of their heads."

Cee rolls her eyes.

"But it *could* get cleared up," I say. "I mean, he could at least give you back what he took." As soon as I say this, I hear how naive I sound, how in denial.

Ken looks amused. "Okay, kid," he says. "Let's go outside. We are grilling for lunch. Get you a hot dog." He stands up, emitting a big groan. "You deserve a hot dog immensus."

"God, Dad, seriously," Cee says, and hearing her say this feels like old times, even though it's nothing like old times and never will be. Cee and I get up, and she walks over to Jay, extends her hand, and pulls him up to standing.

Going outside is like stepping into my old room—so familiar and nice, even though it no longer feels like it belongs to me. Ken is wearing his customary apron, which says I'M NOT OLD I'M JUST MARINATING. Jay turns on the heat lamps. Cee and I light the wood in the fire pit. After, we sit staring at the flames.

"How's your back?" Cee asks Jay.

"Fine," he says.

"How are your ribs?" she asks me.

I feel my rib cage. "You woke 'em up," I say. "Is there a good dojo in Kansas?"

"Fuck if I know," she says. She tucks her hair behind her ear and bites her lower lip.

"Good barbecue, I bet."

She smiles, though it's just to be polite.

"What about getting a scholarship or something and staying here?" I feel stupid for suggesting this, and she doesn't bother to answer or hand me a polite smile.

"Okay, children," Ken says from the grill. "Young adults. Get it while it's hot."

After we eat, Jay and Ken clean up, leaving us to ourselves.

"So how's Breck going?" Cee asks. She looks ahead, her legs propped on the table.

"It's actually good," I say. "I'm having fun. It's weird. A lot has happened."

She lifts her eyebrows. "Like?"

I start to tell her about the kitchen, about Rickie, Nat, and even Brose, but I can sense that she's only pretending to be interested. These are strangers to her, and she must think it's annoying and unfair that I'm not having an absolutely horrible time. I can imagine Mackenzie and the others being the same way—not caring about things that don't involve them. I can also imagine her reporting to them on all of this—"She works as a dishwasher now!" she'd say, and the other girls would be delighted. But it's more than that, I realize. Even now, despite it all, here I am, telling her good news as she's about to pack up and move from everything she has known.

I switch topics and stick to asking questions about her, which makes things okay again. She talks about parties and who hooked up with who, and the new drama between Mackenzie and Kate. The anecdotes are both a relief and an irritation. I guess everyone's the same—once you leave, you're gone.

"So you're not even going to be at school on Wednesday?" I ask. Five days from now.

"Nope," she says.

"So weird. I don't know if I'll be home by then either."

She gets up and walks over to the mini fridge by the grill. She looks back toward the house, pulls out two beers, then walks back to the couch. "Here," she says. "A last hurrah."

She hands me a beer and sits back down. We scoot forward on the couch, preparing to shotgun our cans with our thumbs, something we learned from YouTube. We hold the beers at arm's length, then press our thumbs into the lower part of the cans, puncturing the metal. It took me a while to master this, Cee always telling me that it requires fortitude, calm, and thirst. But now it's easy. I get sprayed in the face, and for the first time today, Cee laughs. We put our mouths on the cans, crack open the tops, and let the beer flow into our mouths. A lot spills out, as usual, but it's more about the process than the brew.

We wipe our mouths with our sleeves and look at one another.

"I'm sorry," I say.

"It's not your fault," she says. "It's not you."

It feels so good to hear her say that, but then it doesn't. Isn't my father a part of me? I'll always carry him in my blood and bones, just like he'll always carry me.

"My dad could go to jail," I say, for the very first time believing it. My father, who art in jail.

"Makes my problems seem not so bad," Cee says, "when you put it that way. I always think of him screwing us over, but he's screwing himself over worse. I'm sorry I just said that."

I put my empty can back on the table. "Is it wrong that I hope he wins?"

She shrugs. "You're looking out for him. And for yourself."

"That's not it—"

"Of course that's it. It's what we're supposed to do."

I sigh and look toward the mini fridge.

"Another?" she asks.

"Yeah, but I want to go slow."

She gets one beer for us to share. "Not too slow. My dad will freak."

The heat lamps make me feel like we're sunbathing. Cold beer, hot sun, her yard of snow like a sea of whitecaps. We take it slow.

From the front seat I watch Ken put his hand on Cee's back and lead her into the house, a small gesture that brings tears to my eyes. I know we won't stay in touch, and unexpectedly, the thought of our friendship coming to an end makes me feel free. I buckle my seat belt, relishing the silence before Jay opens his door, a flush of cold shooting in. We drive out of the neighborhood, and I look upon it as if it's an old childhood place that I haven't seen in years.

There's where Cee and I would cross-country ski—where we found twenty dollars and spent it all on candy. There's the house where Cee and I had to pick Jay up—he was asleep in one of the bedrooms, so drunk he was passed out with his arms sticking up in the air like a zombie. The homes get larger and larger—Zippy's house, Connor and Jax, Arianna and Bailey. I see our house high up on the hill in the distance, overlooking it all. It's strange that I don't even have the urge to drive by. I just want to get home. To our other home.

"What's a bear garden?" I ask, thinking of Ken's explanation. Our dad got himself into a bear garden.

"Beer?" Jay says.

"No," I say. "He said bear."

Jay doesn't answer. We drive in silence, passing homes still lit with Christmas, and then no lights. Just music.

"Dad made the hearing sound routine," Jay says. "This is fucked up. I'm so embarrassed." Jay says this as if just realizing the shame he feels and how much more is in store for us. "This is horrible, Annie."

It's weird to hear him say my name.

"Can't wait to get the hell out of here," he says, his shame leaping into anger.

"You can't *leave*."

"I can leave for Oregon this summer," he says.

"Has your tuition been paid already?" I ask, and he's about to answer, then stops. We've never had to ask about something like tuition before.

We're the only ones on this section of the highway, I realize, framed by the steep mountains, the sharp rocks.

"That's not what I meant anyway," I say. "You can't leave our family. You can't leave this."

"*This* is such bullshit," he says. "He fucked up. He lied to people, he lied to us."

"I know," I say. "If we believe Ken."

He's about to respond, but he doesn't. I wonder if we're thinking the same thing. We know Ken. We know our father. We know what things are supposed to look like and what they're really like. We know who to believe. We just don't want to, and we don't want to say it out loud.

And so we drive the rest of the way in silence. He drops me off at work. I get out without saying good-bye, and he doesn't say anything either. We're holding it in, waiting for the right moment to let it all go.

16

Steak and Rib is packed tonight, and it's early—the happy hour crowd, which to me means people who don't go home to shower. Brose looks stressed out, as he usually is at the beginning of the night. I've never noticed how green his eyes are, how broad his chest. He catches me looking at him, and I swear he scowls. I don't know what his deal is, but I guess he isn't that friendly or sociable with anyone, and I don't know why I'm challenging myself by wanting him to not hate me. I return his look with an amused, pitying look. I've had a shot on top of the shotgun and feel good all over, even in the lobes of my ears. I tamp everything that's happened with Cee and Ken down, way down.

When Nat comes in, I don't look up. The dishwater feels like silk. The Beastie Boys are playing, and earlier Skip came in and said that the Beastie Boys have been playing in this kitchen for more than seventeen years. Maybe longer, but that's when he started working here.

I finish my set of dishes and walk over to Brose. He's slicing ostrich, and the meat looks perfectly medium rare.

"I'd like lipstick in that color," I say, and he looks at my lips, something I didn't intend, but now I intend to use that line another time on someone. Put it in my playbook.

"Dead Ostrich by Revlon," he says, which makes me smile. He stands with his legs far apart.

"Wild Game," I say, looking up from the meat.

"Ready?" Nat says, walking up to the line. Brose shoves it forward.

"Easy, line chef," Nat says, and walks away.

"Guy's such a dick," Brose says.

"Yes, yes, he is," I say.

"I guess you'd know."

I can't read his tone—if it's sympathetic or accusatory. It's embarrassing. How many people know about us?

"I do know." I wish I had something to do. I realize I'm tracing the counter, my fingers gathering salmonella. "Hey, so, what's your deal with me?" I turn to face him, and he gives me a cold, incredulous look, but then it softens under my unwavering stare.

His shoulders relax. His hands rest on the counter. "I don't know," he says. And that's it. We just look at one another, as if we're each trying to solve an equation first. He shrugs. Gets some celery, passes it to me.

"I've got baggage," he says. "And some money concerns, and you just seem to waltz in—take it or leave it, slum it and go."

I dice the celery. "You don't know anything about me." Our tones aren't hostile, I notice, just honest. "I've got baggage, too." He looks me over, amused, but seems to check himself. We dice, dice, dice in a way that's becoming fun and competitive.

"I bet you've got luggage, not baggage," he says.

"Yup," I say. "Coach and Louis Vuitton. The very best."

He keeps his head down, but is smiling. "You want to do something after this?"

"Like what?" I ask.

"We could go find some music somewhere," he says. His expression seems to be carrying a warm joke. "The Gold Pan?"

"Mining for music," I say. "Dancing on peanut shells?"

"Yes," he says, and holds up his arms like his sports team just scored.

"Sure," I say. "But check your baggage."

I go back to my station, my face even warmer. I run my hands under the dishwater and wait for the night to end and begin.

When we're done, Brose holds the kitchen's swinging door and we walk out to the bar. He begins to talk to Forest, and I talk to Rickie.

"Want to go to the Gold Pan with us?" I ask. "Dance on peanut shells?"

"Who's us?" she says.

"Me and Brose." I look down, then up at her, cringing.

"Oh, cute," she says. "Yeah, sure. I'm down." Brose walks to the front of the restaurant, gesturing that he'll wait up there.

"Hey, Annie?" I turn to see Skip behind the bar, pouring a glass of wine for a woman who looks like she's wearing a beaver on her head.

"What?" I say, and can tell that he's taken aback by my

rudeness. I just want to be here without an authority figure like everyone else.

"Maybe head home tonight."

I glance at Jessica, whose boobs are positively demanding to be stared at.

"Maybe," I say.

Rickie elbows me.

"I mean *do*. Do head home tonight."

I give him a look. He's not my dad. My dad doesn't even tell me what to do. No one does. And he just said "do do."

"Nicole should be home in a few hours," he says. "Or maybe sooner."

"Great," I say. "I'll go home." I walk out through the crowded restaurant. It's filled with lots of families tonight. The kind of families that have minivans with stick figure bumper stickers illustrating their abundance.

When we get outside, I tell Brose and Rickie that I need to go home. "You guys go ahead," I say.

"Nah, that's okay," Rickie says. "I could use a night off anyway."

"I have Amazon Prime," I say. "If you guys want to come over and watch something. Nicole's out tonight, so . . . we've got the place for a while."

Brose has his hands in his pockets, and he takes them out and blows into them.

"Sure," he says.

"I'll let you guys do that," Rickie says, and smiles at me as if we're in on something. I roll my eyes, but hope I'm not blushing. I was challenging myself with Brose, and I guess I won. I like him.

It's crept up on me, and now it's here. I'm here, and I've become a person who doesn't like being alone, especially tonight. I want distance from this afternoon—my town and my family. I know I need to look at things up close, but I just don't want to right now.

And so I obey Skip and head home as Annie Town, someone who's never heard of Cee and Ken Rush, Genesee, Aria development, someone who has neither baggage nor luggage. And Jacob Tripp? The developer? She may have met him once or twice. He's her uncle's brother-in-law, a stranger who she knows.

17

I don't know how this happened, but one minute we're watching TV, and the next I'm losing my virginity to Brose. Well, I guess I do know how it happened. What happened was we started to talk about baggage, that stuff we were supposed to leave behind.

"My dad lost his job," Brose told me.

"That's funny," I said. "Mine lost his, too."

He didn't really, but as it turns out, Brose's dad didn't technically lose his job either.

"He did his job, but he didn't get paid for it," Brose said. "Stiffed by this prick. All his staff stiffed, too."

The thought made me feel mortified—that's exactly what my dad's been accused of doing.

"And he works in Denver?" I asked.

"Yup," Brose said. "So that's why I'm working full-time. I'm going to take the semester off, but my dad doesn't know that yet."

I realized I didn't know anything about him. "From college?"

"Yeah, first year. Boulder."

We were watching TV on my bed, upright and innocent. We kept having to pause the movie and ended up never restarting it.

"What about you?" he asked. "What does your dad do?"

"Real estate," I spat out. "Commercial sales."

"Ah," Brose said.

He seemed to be slowly sinking into a gloom the more we talked, and I wanted out of the conversation. I felt so bad about everything too. We were in similar situations and yet not at all. His dad was on the receiving end of something. Mine, the possible executioner. His circumstances led him to get a job, stop college, share the stress. Mine led me to get a job for fun and buy hippie clothing that costs the same as my designer clothes. I felt like a fraud, like a spoiled princess, like the girl Brose assumed me to be. And so I kissed him, and then things got intense, but good intense, my worries transforming into pure sensation, and then I stopped thinking about anything at all . . .

And now here we are, lying on the bed, moving back and forth. It's like I'm the one who could go to jail and am trying to do as much as I can before I'm locked up. Going home again might feel that way. We won't want to leave our rooms. We'll be treated like felons. And why am I thinking about this now?

I look at the ceiling, wincing because it hurts and he's lying on my collarbone. I don't want to say anything, because he's moving gently and seems to be in a happy place. *I'm a different person now.* A different girl, but this makes me feel like I'm in an artsy film about mental illness or young sexuality, and so I try not to clear my thoughts. But that doesn't work. I keep thinking about how I got here. I mean, I like Brose, but this is excessive. What would Cee or my brother's friends think of me now? I can't wait to tell Rickie, which makes me imagine her and Tamara, which makes me close my eyes and feel him, in a good way. It's a feeling like this is something I'd like to do again.

I make some sort of noise.

"Are you okay?" Brose stops and looks down at me, his face close.

"Yeah," I say. He moves slowly. It's much nicer with the space between us. "Yes."

"I like you," he says.

"That's good," I say.

"I'm not just saying that," he says. "I always have. Despite not wanting to."

"I know," I say. "Oh god."

"What?" His brows are furrowed. He looks like he just bit his lip.

"Nothing," I say. "It just felt nice. Just then."

He smiles, bites his lip, and looks down at my stomach and begins to rev back up. He's getting strong and creative with his thrusts and then he looks at me, his kind face looking pained, like he just found out his grandma died. He lets out a constrained whimper-grunt and falls back on top of me.

I let out a hum. I just don't know how to do this or what I'm supposed to say. I don't know if that was all it was supposed to be for me. I feel like there's more road ahead. His breath is warm on my neck. His hands slowly release their grip on me. There's a penis in me right now. How long will it be there? Do I take it out?

He rolls off of me and I look down quickly to make sure the condom is still on him.

He turns his head toward me and grins like we both just finished a race on a bicycle built for two. I feel like I need a doctor. I kind of want to try it again, but I kind of feel like I'm using him just to get some steps under my belt, things I can check off. But no. I'm not using him. I just feel safe with him. Like I have nothing to fear tomorrow. I roll on top of him and let out a little shriek, which makes him laugh and run his hand through my hair.

"Brose," I say. "Where did your name come from?"

"Short for Ambrose," he says.

"I've never met an Ambrose before." We kiss, and it's so soft, so loving, and then the door opens.

My heart seems to throttle me. I fly off of him, and he drops off the side of the bed.

"Holy shit attack!" Jay says.

"What the hell!" I say.

"What do you mean what the hell?" he says. "What the hell to you?"

"You didn't tell me you had a boyfriend," Brose says, in a loud whisper by my side.

"I'm her brother, dude!" Jay yells. "And my car is in the driveway, geniuses. I'm only here 'cause I thought you were crying again, but I obviously heard something else. God, I'm going to barf."

Brose mutters something from the ground.

Jay shakes his head and puts his hands on his hips. He looks at me, then looks up at the ceiling. "And you are?" he says.

Brose sits up to show his face. "I'm Brose."

Jay appraises his face, then looks at me and shakes his head. "Hi, Brose, I'm Jay. Nice to meet you."

"Get out of here!" I say.

"Can you give us a moment to change?" Brose says.

"What's going on?" Skip sticks his head in.

"Oh my god," I say. I pull the covers up higher.

"Brose?" Skip says, and Brose drops down once again, hitting his head on the bedside table.

"Ow! Skip is here," he whispers loudly. "Why is he here?"

"Because he lives here," I say. "He's my uncle."

"What? Are you serious? Why didn't you tell me that?"

"How have you not known that this whole time?"

Skip and Jay are just watching me in disbelief.

"I don't know! I was focused on my work!"

"Get off the floor," Skip says, his voice calm and threatening.

"Hey, guy," Jay says. "I have an aunt I can bring in here if you want. And I could call up some other family members while I'm at it."

"Get off the floor, Brose," Skip says again.

I feel like I'm in *Once Upon a Time in the West*. Skip looks like Henry Fonda, his sad eyes focused and intense.

"Please, not yet," Brose says. "Not now."

Skip releases a kind of roar. He hits the wall with his fist, then leaves the room.

"He left," I say. Brose scrambles to dress, and I see him put the condom in his pocket. He puts on his shoes, jacket, gloves, hat.

"Got everything there, bud?" Jay asks.

"I think so. There's my scarf." He picks up his scarf that I took off of him and threw on the shelf. I thought it was so cute that he was wearing a scarf.

"Bye," he says to me on the bed. Then he lowers his voice. "That was really great. Except for now." He makes to lean down and kiss me, but looks at Jay and clumsily pats my head. He walks by Jay and does a kind of respectful bowing gesture.

"So sorry," he says.

When he gets out to the hall, I hear Skip say, "Show up early tomorrow, Ambrose."

"Yes, sir," Brose says. "I didn't know. I respect Annie very much, sir. I wasn't using her or anything."

"Jesus, Brose," Skip says.

"I just . . . She's . . . different from the other girls . . . I mean not *the* other girls. There are no other girls. It's just . . . she's very candid, sensitive, not to touch, but . . . God. Sorry. I just mean, she's very . . . giving. She's not like—"

Jay covers his mouth with his hand, covering a huge laughing smile, and I can't hear the rest of what Brose is saying, even though I'm straining to hear every word.

"Shut up," I say.

"And I swear," I hear him say, "I had no idea you were related."

"Yup, that's Annie," Skip says. "Annie Town."

I can't believe he's still continuing the Annie Town thing. As if it matters. A niece is a niece, awkward no matter what. Jay is practically crying with his hand still over his mouth.

"I'm going to tape that hand to your mouth, weedwacker," I say.

"This is just quality goods," Jay says. "Oh my god. I should stay home more often."

I sit up, feeling less like I've had sex than been operated on and my family's come in to check on me.

"Wipe the grin off your fat face," I say.

"I'm just taken aback," he says. "I didn't know you had a gentleman friend. Or that you're . . . uh . . . active."

"I'm not active—that was my first time."

He holds his hands up. "Please. Say no more. Shit, should I call Mom?"

"No!"

"I mean for guidance, like, if you need a subscription or prescription or whatever—things are bad enough as it is. You don't want to get pregnant—"

"Get out!" I throw Nicole's stuffed duck at him. It lands near his feet. He picks it up by its neck and brings it back to me.

"Look, I'm choking the chicken." He holds it by the neck.

"He's a duck, jackass!"

"Which reminds me—there's nothing wrong with self-love. It's only natural to explore yourself—"

"Out, scum sack! Out!" I scream, and Skip comes back in.

"Girls are scary when they're mad," Jay says.

"No shit," Skip says. He has two beers in his hand.

"Can you guys leave my room now?" I ask. I feel more naked than naked. Even though it's warm, it's like I'm shivering.

"I can't leave," Skip says. "We need to talk. We need to address this."

"Is that beer for me?" Jay asks.

Skip looks at the beers as if forgetting he's holding them. "No," he says. "The second one's just . . . in my queue. But you may as well have it. Have a case! I've failed the parenting exam."

He really does look like he's failed something he was really working hard at. I almost want to comfort him. But I'm naked. And I'm about to get lectured.

"Where's Aunt Nicole?" Jay asks.

"She's at GNO, girls' night out, or moms' night out, which means she's probably drunk, because she hates GNO. I told her I have it under control. I have you guys under control. Wrong!" He looks up, the dazed look hardening. "Look at you kids. The dynamic duo. I'm at a loss."

Jay and I look at one another.

"Damn it!" Skip says. "Brose. Damn punk. I did him a favor, and . . . Jesus, Nicole's going to annihilate me. Don't tell her anything. Not yet. Okay?" He exhales violently. "I need a sec. Annie, get dressed. Meet outside in the shed. I need to move around or something. Goddamn it." He walks out, shaking his head.

"So busted," Jay says.

I walk outside fully dressed with my ski coat and a blanket wrapped around me. Skip's in the shed, sawing something. When I get closer, I see a blueprint of a crib tacked to the wall.

"Hey," I say.

He stops sawing, takes a drink of his Pabst, and looks back.

"Hey," he says. Then he looks behind me, and I turn to see Jay loafing up with his hands in his pockets.

"Jesus, you don't need to be here," I say.

Jay shrugs. "I want to be here."

I let it go, thinking it might be less awkward this way.

The shed smells like sawdust, which always gives me a good feeling, like something's on the verge of being. Skip sits on a tree stump. I see some more along the wall and figure I should pull up a stump, too. I grab one, but it doesn't budge, so I just sit on it where it is. Jay is looking at the picture of the crib.

"I don't know what to say," Skip says. "We need to address this, but I really don't know how to go about it."

"Yeah," I say, not knowing what else I can add. My body feels different. It's reminding me that something has happened to it. I almost feel like it's another person that I'm trying to hide.

"I hope you know to be safe," Skip says. "You know—to use protection, not just for pregnancy but, I don't know, warts and such."

Jay and I exchange looks and cringe.

"Don't worry," I say. "I'm not there yet."

I feel good about this lie. He looks so incredibly relieved.

"Good," he says. "Okay. Okay. It's not bad. It's just . . . There's a sweet phase. Don't go too fast."

He's addressing the floor, so he can't see our bewildered faces. "Don't bypass the sweet phase. You're young. There's this innocent exploration. But then . . . well, it kind of ends, and—" Now he looks up. "I'm responsible for you, Annie. I don't want you to get hurt. This goes for both of you."

"Okay," I say. "I'm sorry." And I truly am. To hear him say he's responsible for us warms me up inside. I can't imagine my father saying something like that, or working in a shed with a beer and sawdust. It's so peaceful here, a place where even though you're alone, you probably don't feel alone.

"I know I'm not covering this completely," he says. "Again, I'm kind of new at this. But Brose shouldn't be here when adults aren't here. You shouldn't have boys over." He looks at Jay, unsure if this is a practical rule, and then he seems to give up.

"I know you're smart," he says to me. "And I'm sure your parents have already gone over all of this."

Nope. Never. The only thing my mom said about puberty was that I should try to stay thin so I wouldn't get my period too early and stop growing. Mira helped me when I actually got my period, and the rest was covered in school.

"Hell, maybe this is just fine and dandy, then," he says, getting no response from us. "But in my house, I don't want boys over without my knowledge. Got it?"

"Got it," I say. "I'm sorry."

He picks up the jigsaw—at least that's what I think it is. "And don't tell Nicole about this either," he says, gesturing to the crib. "She'll think I'm jinxing it."

"That's sweet, man," Jay says. "This is cool." Jay walks over to the frame and runs his hand along it. "A father's gift made with his hands. That's something."

His voice is serious, and I know we're both thinking of Dad, trying to remember him making anything. There was that time when he made wine at one of his company retreats.

"Your dad's given you some pretty good stuff, too, I bet," Skip says.

True. He's given us more than most kids will ever have, and yet nothing like this sweet crib, a place to sleep and dream.

Jay and I don't say anything.

"What would he do?" Skip says. "Your dad."

"About what?" I ask.

"About you," he says. His eyes are kind, searching. I want to help him make this crib. I want to be good to him.

"He'd ground her," Jay says, not meanly. "He'd have Mom deal with it."

I shrug. He's right.

"What would he do if it was you?" Skip asks Jay. "What if he caught you with a girl?"

"I don't know," Jay says. "I mean—he gave me condoms once."

"Okay, then," Skip says, and wipes his hands on his jeans. "Annie, you're not grounded, but we need to go over some house rules—I might think of more things, so this isn't over, and I think we'll need to talk more about sex."

He yells this last word as if forcing it off his tongue and then goes back to sawing wood. "We'll talk more tomorrow. I'll come up with some . . . guidelines. And I'll need to share this with Nicole."

He saws harder, and it seems he's done with us. Jay tilts his head toward the house and heads across the yard. I get up, mumble a good-night.

"Annie?" Skip says, but doesn't turn to face me.

"Yeah?" I say, and then add, "Yes?" to be more polite.

"Brose isn't . . . He's not right for you."

A tinge of defensiveness tints the remorse I was just feeling. "Because he's in college?" I ask. Or because he's hardworking, moral, from an uncorrupted family.

149

"Yes," Skip says. "And he's . . . he's got stuff going on."

"I know," I say, kind of smugly. I'm sure I know way more about it than he ever will, but it's hard to take a tone with Skip. He's such a good guy. I'm sure he's just looking out for both of us.

"He told me his dad lost his job and doesn't know that Brose is taking time off Boulder to work."

Skip nods, starts to speak, then holds back. He takes a sip of his beer. "I've known his family a long time," he says. "Besides, you're not here for much longer. You wouldn't want to, you know, get attached."

"Right," I say. "Good night, then." I walk back to the house.

I get into bed. I keep hearing Brose's voice, how he told Skip that I'm giving and that I'm different. I pull up the covers and close my eyes. I think about the secret crib, and I can't believe I was ever so small or that there was a time when my parents didn't know who I was or who I'd be: a woman. I think about Skip saying I'd be leaving soon and how that gave me a surprising punch of sadness; how Skip asked Jay what my dad would do if it were him getting caught with a girl. For the first time in my life, I was treated the same as my brother.

18

The next morning, everything changes, or everything is about to change. I can tell when I get home and walk through the front door that Nicole was waiting for me and she's angry, which makes me defensive and angry too.

"Where were you?" she asks.

I close the door, then hold up my two bags of groceries. "King Soopers. I wanted to make eggs Benedict."

"You need to tell us where you're going." She looks tired, and there's a snarl in her hair on the side of her head that looks like a little cactus. I can't believe she's my mom's sister. Right now she looks like someone who'd be eligible for an ambush makeover.

I put my bags on the counter. "Okay. I'll tell you where I'm going."

She looks in a bag as if she doesn't believe I went to the store. "And I think you shouldn't go anywhere. Skip told me you had a visitor last night."

"Yeah, and he said I wasn't grounded." I take out the spinach and wash it in the sink.

"That was before talking to me." She starts emptying the dishwasher, so we're standing side by side. She reaches up to the cabinets to put the mugs away. I have the urge to grab her skinny arms and squeeze them.

"What are you grounding me for?" I ask calmly. "Having sex? You and Skip do that all the time, I'm sure."

She drops a pile of forks into the drawer. "You're grounded for saying that about me and Skip—that is very disrespectful, and we don't do it all the time. Jesus. On certain days we do, and it's none of your business. And, wait, you had sex?" She slams the silverware drawer shut. I think I hear the breath coming out of her nostrils.

"No," I lie.

"You're grounded for drinking, and bringing strangers in the house, and for—I didn't know where you were just now, so for that."

"I didn't know those rules," I say.

"Well, now you know." She opens the drawer again, dropping in more utensils.

"Now you blow," I mumble.

"What?"

I leave the groceries and walk toward my room.

"Please pick up after yourself," she calls.

"I always pick up after myself and Jay and you." I turn to face her.

She has this weird expression, like she's angry but doesn't want me to go.

"You never ask Jay to clean up. You never bother him when he comes home late. You just don't like me . . . or my father, and you're jealous of my mother."

"Jealous?" she says, gripping the counter. "You spoiled—

152

you—if you only knew . . . Ow! I was biting my tongue, and I really bit my tongue!"

"You have sharp incisors. You should get them sawed down."

"What is your problem?" she asks. "Where does this all come from?"

"What is your problem?" I ask. "Where does it come from for you?"

We both stare at one another in disbelief. It's a good question. We're at a standstill.

"You said, 'if I only knew,'" I say. "If I only knew what?"

She takes a deep breath and puts both hands on the counter. "Where to begin. If you only knew that I'm protecting you. I think you should stay away from Brose, for one. Two, if you only knew how much I love your mother. I'd do anything for her, and I have. And I do like you. Sort of." She looks down and smiles.

"Are you going to tell my mom?" I ask. The thought of her knowing makes me feel a deep shame. She'd be so disgusted with me, not for being with a guy, but being with a guy like Brose. She'd only see a scruffy college dropout.

"I'll tell her in a heartbeat if you fuck with me," Nicole says. She crosses her arms in front of her. She is such a fit human. She's like a caribou.

"You're not technically grounded," she says. "Okay?"

"Okay," I say.

"But tonight I'd like you to come home." She continues to unload the dishes. "I highly recommend it."

"Isn't that being grounded?" I say.

"No. Because I'm asking you to stay home. And today I'd like you to hang out with one of us. Skip's way out in Sanford picking up fish. I'm going running. So I guess you're going running, too."

"I don't know how."

"You put one foot in front of the other quickly. Get dressed."

"I don't have runner clothes," I say.

"Uh-oh," she sings. "You're fucking with me."

I look at myself in Nicole's bathroom mirror. I'm wearing her clothes: running tights and a long-sleeved sweat-wicking shirt. Or so says the label. Both items are tight. Both items are yellow. I look like a short giraffe. I open her drawers, just like I'd do in my mom's bathroom, but in there I'd slather her wrinkle cream onto my face and hands and spritz her perfume into my hair. I don't want to use Nicole's stuff, though. She doesn't have nearly as much as my mom.

I take one more look at my ridiculous self before going on this ridiculous run and then something in the garbage can catches my eye. It looks like a thermometer, but then I see the box next to it. It's a pregnancy test. I turn to leave then pivot back to look again. I take the box out of the trash to see how to read it, then I use the box to flip the stick over. Two lines positive. One line negative. There's one blue line.

I imagine her in this bathroom as I am now, looking at this stick, and something—her hope—sinking, then disappearing. How many times did she check it? I wonder. How long did she stare at it? Or, knowing Nicole, I could see her looking at the results, tossing the stick, washing her hands, and putting on her running shoes, tricking herself into being okay. *Knowing Nicole*.

I know Aunt Nicole, I realize, and something in me sinks a little too. I feel so absolutely sorry for her.

I walk outside. The sky is wrapped up in a thick gray cloud, and it seems to heave a bit. Everything is so quiet today, as if the landscape is waiting patiently for whatever these clouds have in store for it.

Nicole and her friend wait for me on the road. Her friend has a double stroller with huge wheels.

"You want Giraffey or Mum Mums?" she asks the babies. "Bookie?"

One of the babies furrows her brow like she's incredibly angry or pooping or both. "Okay, Bookie is making you upset," she says, then shakes her head and looks up at me.

"This is my niece, Annie," Nicole says. "Annie, Tanya."

"Hi there," Tanya says. She's really chirpy, and her eye contact is forceful and intense.

"Hello," I say.

She has black curly hair and pale, freckled skin. "These are the twins," she says. "Lily and Rose." She aims the stroller at me. "Can you say 'hi,' friends?" She does sign language to the babies, but they just stare into space, because they're babies.

"Cute outfits," I say. They wear matching onesies that look like sheepskin. I wish I had one in my size. I'd put it on and watch movies all day. Maybe I'd go find a flock of sheep—see if they noticed I wasn't truly one of them.

Tanya says in a baby voice meant to give me the illusion that her babies are talking, "We got them at Marty's. BOGO."

Nicole looks away, possibly embarrassed that this is her friend.

"Bogo?" I ask, snapping my tight pants against my leg.

"Buy One Get One Free!" Tanya says, again with the baby voice.

"That's BOGOF," I say, and Nicole seems to stifle a laugh.

"Should we go?" She presses something on her watch, which makes me nervous, like I'm in PE.

"Let's do this!" Tanya yells, and I'm startled by the sound of her sudden adult voice, squeak free and gravelly deep. And then they're off, like—bam!—a couple of cheetahs. They don't start with a light jog either. They basically gallop out of the gates, and I feel like a cartoon waddling after them, duck-like. I'm in shape from skating, but this is different. I don't run. I've never been a good runner. I follow them out of the neighborhood to the trail across the street. I almost turn back around, but then keep telling myself, *At that rock up ahead I can stop*, but then I pass the rock and think, *At that shadow up ahead I can stop*, and then I pass the shadow and various other landmarks and find that my legs don't feel like they're moving through banks of snow anymore. Still, these are old ladies I'm running with, and they're far ahead. I see them, I see them, I see them, and then I don't, and I'm alone with my breath and the mountain, so poised and regal alongside me.

When I round the corner, Nicole's there with the stroller, and she's holding a fussy baby, who looks awkward in her arms. She holds her under the armpits, and the baby kicks in space.

When I stop, I lean over to take a few breaths, hoping I don't yak or keel over. I haven't exercised in so long. It's been wonderful.

"Here's your giraffe," Nicole says to the baby. "Giraffey."

I look up, thinking that she's talking about me—the giraffe

has arrived—but she's holding the baby close to her now and shaking a plastic giraffe in her face. Then she puts that down and shakes a tube of Puffs.

"I love those things," I say, even though they look kind of repulsive to me at this moment.

"Did you see a pacifier?" Nicole asks. "That one dropped it." She points at a baby.

"I can't breathe," I say.

"Tanya went to look for it on a side trail we took. This one started screaming, so I picked it up. I should have left it alone."

The baby starts to head butt Nicole. "She's trying to nurse," I say.

Nicole looks down at her chest. "Well, she's shit out of luck."

I think of the pregnancy test and wish I didn't know about it. "Here," I say. I hold out my arms and Nicole hands her to me. I cradle her close and put my finger into her mouth. She closes her eyes and sucks, then opens her eyes again. There's wonderment in her eyes like I'm a gigantic gem.

"Which one is this?" I ask. Her eyelashes are like little whiskers.

"No idea. Some kind of flower." Nicole walks closer to us. She touches the baby's little fist. "Look at you. You're good at this."

"It worked with Sammy," I say.

A few flakes of snow drift by. I look up, and the clouds are still brewing. I love that snow starts like this, a passing whisper, and then when more comes down, it sounds the same. I've never seen something so powerful be so quiet.

"You can teach me all the tricks," Nicole says.

I look for sadness in her eyes, that a little item from the

drugstore didn't change her life today when she wanted it to. Nothing to fill her bank, just an invisible, not-really-a-loss loss.

"School starts soon."

"Right," she says. I'm about to put the flower child back when Nicole says, "So, I know at this time in your life, you have desires." I keep my eyes on the baby in the nook of my arm. "I get it. I've been there before."

I look at her out of the corner of my eye. She has her hands on her waist like she's really considering something there on the ground.

"It's good to feel and desire and . . . feel, before it all goes numb down there. Wait, strike that."

I look up, but she's looking away, up to the mountain.

"It's natural to . . . have urges. But you have to be careful."

I mumble some noise to show my acceptance. This lecture is so abrupt. I'm wearing tights and have a finger in a strange baby's mouth. I take it out, feeling suddenly lurid. Fortunately she doesn't cry.

"You're new in town," Nicole says. "It's flattering, I know. So many guys, you get pounced—god, I remember that—but um, take it easy, you don't need to go all the way. You don't want to be one of those . . . And even if you don't . . . do it, like, do it, do it, that doesn't make everything else okay. I mean it's okay, but you're young, and you have to watch your reputation. God. I just said that. I'm a feminist, so part of me wants to say—have at it! Strike that again."

Oh my god. I really want to put this baby down and run out of here. Or walk. Or get a ride. I'd really like a ride and some water and a onesie.

"It's just that I saw this thing on *20/20* where all these young girls are . . ."

She makes the tongue-in-cheek sign for a blow job, and I think my face may look either drained of all color or stained red like a rooster's wattle.

"I mean, they think that's innocent, and that's not good either. Without love. Or not love, necessarily. It's never really an act of love. But girls think because it's not sex, that it's fine. And it is, but . . . um . . . at such a young age, or any age, you want respect. And reciprocation. Oh god." She lets out a big sigh.

"Yeah, I've heard," I say. "My friend kind of said the same thing." My face flushes again. "I just wanted to try it, I mean, try . . . stuff."

I catch her smile, but she quickly does away with it. She looks on the verge of saying something, but seems to think better of it.

"Why stay away from Brose?" I ask. "He seems like a nice guy to me."

"He's very nice," she says, almost thoughtful. "But he's in college, and . . . you guys have different lives."

I give her the baby, whose face is morphing into discontentment, and now Nicole's attention is on this child and not me.

"What do I do?" she says as the baby starts to make pre-cries, thank god. Cry us out, please. Drown us.

"Rock her a bit," I say. "Remember the five *S*'s. Swing, put on side, shush, suck, swaddle."

She rocks the baby on its side.

"Now go, 'Shhh, shhh, shhh,' right into her ear. It's supposed to be like being in the womb." Just the three *S*'s are working now, and she looks up at me, full of embarrassed pride.

"We have some good monitors if you want them," I say. "For when . . . you're ready."

"What?" she says. It's so cute, her confident gaze at the baby, watching her give in to joy.

"Baby monitors," I say. "I noticed some in my room. Or, the room I'm using. We have some better ones."

"Oh god," she says. "Yeah, those were a gift. I miscarried last year; that's why I have them. It's also why I have these—" She looks around then whispers, "Sucky mom friends—god they're horrible. They talk about what their babies eat, like, all the time! What they eat, what they've done. They clapped their hands! They can sit up! I mean, big deal. And look at this outfit." She holds the baby upright, and the baby smiles, all gums. "I would never demean my baby this way."

She puts her back in the stroller, and the baby looks very alert and happy. "Anyway, I joined this moms group when I thought I was going to be a mom, but I'm not a mom. And I still have the monitors. So stupid."

"It's not stupid," I say. The wind hits my sweaty back. It feels nice to be outside. I actually feel like I could run again. "I'm going to be so sore," I say. "I haven't moved like this in a long time."

"Soreness is key," Nicole says. "Proof."

"Yeah, I feel kind of good." I look behind me and then ahead. We covered a lot, and there's still so much more to go. We stand together in this field of ice and dead grass, my aunt and I. I'm relieved that the baby—some sort of flower—didn't cry when she was put back into her stroller. I hope Nicole felt that she accomplished something.

19

That night I go to work with a feeling of peace. It's like I'm a confidante, an adult, someone to be trusted and taken seriously. It's a strange sensation. Even though I've kind of gotten in trouble here, I guess it feels good to be looked at.

The kitchen is slow and quiet, which is disappointing. Brose isn't here, and no one's doing shots or playing music. Even Skip isn't here, which is odd. I'm anxious, like not enough is happening. When you have crazy nights, it feels like a letdown when the others aren't so crazy. I have nothing to do after and can't imagine just sitting at home, especially after last night. It's like I need to be with him.

"What's going on tonight?" I ask Rickie when she drops off a load of dishes. I scrape all the food off. Meat, potatoes, salad, crab legs.

"That would have made some cold hobo really happy," she says. "I don't know what's going on. I think some people are going to cruise at Corboy's later. I need to go home, though. Tomorrow's the Snow Sculpture first showing. My parents get all into it."

"That's cute," I say, wondering what it would be like to have parents like that, parents who made ice sculptures together for the town contest. I mean, that is innocence.

"I have to remember that it's cute," she says, and looks around the kitchen. "It's so classic that Skip basically put Brose on a time-out. He grounded Brose."

"So that's why he's not here?"

"Yeah, Skip told him to not come in."

I look down. I told her what happened, and I'm not sure what she thinks.

"You're like Romeo and Juliet," she says. "Broseo and Anniette. Banned from one another."

"Yeah," I say, and it kind of does feel like that. Both Skip and Nicole told me to stay away from him, but it's not like he's that much older than me. Do they not want me around him because they know it would upset my parents? Would Nat—asshole, but rich and the *right* kind of boy—make the cut? Would I be allowed to see *him*? The thought makes me furious.

"You're welcome to come over and just chill," Rickie says.

"I think I'm grounded," I say, "but I guess girls don't count."

Rickie rolls her eyes, but smiles. "Yeah, girls are sweet and innocent. We have no interest in sex." She winks, and I bite my lower lip, thinking that maybe I *would* be allowed over to Rickie's. She isn't Brose. She can't get me pregnant. This makes me smile to myself, but then I see Tamara walk in, and she looks at me smiling and cringes like I have bird shit on my face.

I load the rest of the dishes, help Pablo clean up, then I clock out. I walk outside with Rickie. The air is sharp and clear, making me more alert and not ready to go home. I ask Rickie for Brose's number. I gave mine to him and am surprised he hasn't been in touch yet. I plug his number into my phone, prepared to be reckless like Juliet and meet him, but Rickie nudges me.

"Look," she says. "It's your foster mom."

"Damn it."

Nicole is walking through the lot unsteadily. What is she doing? Her hair looks pretty, flowing out of a white beanie.

"Hey there, Aunt Nicole," I say.

"Niece Annie!" she says, walking toward us, then coming to an abrupt stop. "What's up, girlies? What the hell is going on?!"

Rickie and I exchange looks.

"You heading home?" she asks. "I think so, right? Since you're *not supposed to go out*." For some reason this is amusing to her. "Come on. I'll give you a ride."

"Guess I'm going home," I say to Rickie, and feel caught and anxious, not quite ready to accept this. There must be a way for me to meet him tonight. "Good luck tomorrow." I imagine Rickie and her family creating something so cold and solid together.

"Good luck." She takes my hand, gives it a little shake. I feel her fingers glide against my own, and then she lets go.

Inside the car, Nicole fumbles through her purse. "My keys are always lost, always."

"They're on your lap," I say, and she honks out a laugh.

"Why didn't you tell me?" She hits my leg with her fist.

"I didn't know that's what you were looking for."

She leans back into her seat. "Maybe you should drive."

I blow into my hands for warmth. "I'm not good at it. And I'm not supposed to drive if it's snowing."

"It's not far," she says. "Great. I've just jinxed it. Now we can't drive."

"We can walk," I say.

"Fuck that noise. It's cold."

I hold back my laughter and look over at her. She's like a teenager. She looks to the street, and something catches her eye.

"Horses!" she says.

We sit in the horse-drawn carriage, a blanket over our laps. The whole town is quiet tonight. Ribbons decorate the lampposts. I feel like I'm in a Christmas story and want to snuggle into an older time without cars. I text Brose: **You around tonight?**

"There's nothing that will take you away from the . . . crap of life better than a horse-drawn carriage," Nicole says. "The romantic clip-clop of hooves will transport you to a Breckenridge past, rich with adventure and gold and whores and black sheep. Clip-clop!"

The driver looks back at her, and Nicole rolls her eyes.

"Is that from a pamphlet?" I ask.

"Pretty much," she says. "Hey, why don't you drive? Isn't that what all teens want?"

"My mom thinks it's dangerous, so—"

"That's stupid," she says. "Jay does it. You can too. Equality. And what about when he goes to college? Who's going to drive you to school . . . school and the malls? What if you still live with us? I can't drive back and forth."

"I won't be," I say. At least I think I won't be. School starts in four days. "So, did you paint the town tonight or what?"

"No, I went down to see Skip—was he there just now? I forgot to look."

"No. He never came in."

"Hope he's okay. Oh my god, what if he's hurt, or dead! Anyway, we kind of celebrate every time I get a negative pregnancy test. I got one. When I went earlier to the restaurant, he wasn't there, so I went out alone."

"I'm sorry," I say, feeling weird about already knowing.

"It's fine," she says.

"You celebrate?"

"Yes, weird, I know. We have a drink, celebrate the two of us, because it won't always be that way. That kind of thing. God, we've had a lot of celebrations."

"That's a good attitude," I say. I'm lulled by the rhythm of the horse's steps, the bounce of the carriage.

"Well, mostly I complain the whole night—like, 'I'm such an infertile louse' or 'I've gotten pregnant three times before, why can't I do it again' kind of thing." She yawns.

"You've been pregnant three times?"

"Yeah, yeah, two miscarriages, then before, long time ago, I was twenty-two, and my egg got pregnant, not me, so I guess that doesn't count. Kinda counts, though."

The driver, perhaps hearing us, starts to whistle.

"You gave your eggs to someone?" I ask.

"Yes," she says, yawning again, loudly. Her eyes water.

"Like, to make money?"

"No, no, I gave them . . . to a friend." She looks to her side of the street, where someone is selling roasted cashews.

"Must have been a good friend," I say, thinking of Cee, what I would have done for her. I don't think I would have given her my future children.

"Yes," Nicole says. "She was." The way she says this makes me think that it's no longer the case.

"Have you done IVF?" I ask.

She looks over, maybe surprised I know what IVF is. Oh, I know, all right. If IVF is in your family, it's your life too.

"No," she says. "Too many twins. I don't want multiples—they're everywhere now. Like the flower girls. Tanya did it. Plus, it's expensive."

She steadies herself, grabbing my wrist. "I hate when moms want to have a kid right after their first so their kid can have a buddy. There are so many people on this damn planet—I mean, they'll have a friggin' buddy. And so many of them just decide. They just say, 'I'm going to have a second one now.' And then they do."

Her words tumble forth. I think how jealous of my mom she must have been, having Jay, then me so quickly after.

"Listen to me," she says. "I don't even like babies. I actually hate them. The twins? Gardenia and whoever? I felt nothing. And I'm supposed to, right?" She grabs my elbow as if she's falling.

"Then why do you want one?" I ask.

She sighs, and I wait for her to answer. "It's been so long since we've been trying, I don't even remember. It's what comes next."

"You want a little buddy," I say.

"I want this place"—she gestures to everything around us, the mountain, the hotels, this snow-globe life—"to mean something. I want it to be our home. Skip and I have been doing the same things for a long time."

I must look confused.

"Imagine nothing changing in your life, never graduating. I want to graduate. I know you can change your life in other ways, but I want the baby to be the way, and it's just part of life, putting down roots, having collaborators. I look at your mom and like what she has. I'm not into kids, but I'll love the baby after I've met her. I hope. I'm kind of banking on it."

"You will," I say. "She'll be yours."

Something passes over her face, and she seems to be holding something back. I think of my family as collaborators, but it just fills me with a bad feeling. What have we collaborated on? What have we done together? I feel guilty and dirty.

"Right now I don't even see a baby," she says. "I see time running out. I'm forty." She looks over at me. "You're so young. You're so pretty."

I roll my eyes.

"You must hear that all the time," she says. "Sorry. That's not all you are."

I tuck my lips in, shy. "My mom had a hard time, too," I say, trying to comfort her. "I guess Jay was easy, but it was harder for me, and she did IVF a bunch of times for Sammy. I know you're not close, but . . . you could always talk to her."

Nicole looks perplexed. The carriage comes to a stop at the end of Main Street.

"Hope you've enjoyed the romantic clip-clop of horseshoes," the driver says.

"Will you turn into French Creek?" Nicole asks.

"The horse stops here," he says.

"I'll pay more for the horse to keep going. Or she will. She's rich."

The driver looks at his watch, and then the horse continues on.

It's strange when we enter the dark residential neighborhood, like we've really traveled into the past. The horse looks sad, walking with its blinders. It's funny that it's less afraid when it can't see as much. We've been quiet for a while, both in our own heads. I am at peace.

"That doesn't make sense," she says.

"Hmm?" I say, looking ahead so I don't see the cars in people's driveways. I want to pretend I'm in the past.

"You and Jay are so close in age," she says. "How'd she have a hard time with you? Didn't seem hard. You came right after. Not like she tried for ten years."

"I never thought about that."

She laughs harshly. "And did she tell you Jay was easy?"

I give her a conspiring grin. "I think it was her way of saying he was an accident."

"He wasn't an accident," she says. "And he definitely wasn't easy. Nothing was easy about it."

I realize she's really stewing, and I wonder what I've said wrong.

"Okay. So, what, she lied?"

"Yes. She did."

"It's kind of an odd thing to lie about," I say.

"Your mother has always hidden things unnecessarily. Always. I mean, look at you now. You're here. Hiding."

I stare ahead.

"I cannot believe she told you that Jay came easy. Just wham, bam, thank you, ma'am. What's the point of telling you that?"

"I get you're sensitive about—"

"I'm not fucking sensitive."

"Whoa!" I say, my heart beating fast. The horse stops.

"Not you, Pandemonium," the driver says, and the horse resumes after a cluck. "How much longer?"

"Just look for the Santa on the Harley that blink-blinks all night long!" she says.

I see the Santa up ahead.

"My mom always said that you resented her, that you never wanted to know us—I finally get it—"

"Your mom made it a point for me not to know you. I'd offer to babysit all the time. I'd come over to see Jay after he was born. I'd invite you over and send all kinds of crap that your mom shoved in a closet because it didn't fit in with her decor. Like that duck that's in your room now—Ping. I gave him the book, *The Story About Ping*, along with that duck, which became his absolute favorite. She shoved it in the closet. I took it back for days when he'd 'visit'—yeah, like that ever happened. I wanted to be your cool aunt. I was excited. I had plans. I was fine with everything!"

"She didn't want you around because you imbibe, and you had an eating disorder and have a drug problem. That's why—"

"I imbibe? I have a drug problem? My goodness, I smoke a little pot, the whole town does. She should, too! And everyone has an eating disorder when they're young."

"She says you can't get pregnant because of all that stuff," I say. The Santa is getting brighter. I want to stay on this horse, but alone. I text Brose again: Please. I need you. Can u meet?

"You've got to be kidding!" she says. "She said that? She actually said that?"

"Yes," I say, and feel kind of bad about it. I soften my look and am about to say I'm sorry, but smile when I notice her rogue

169

eyebrow, and then I freeze. My smile falls. Her intense anger at my mom for lying about Jay, their estranged relationship, her selfless, unbelievable favor for a "friend." Oh my god.

"It was for my mom," I say.

She rubs her eyes. "What?"

The driver starts whistling again. *Take me home, country roads.* I try to speak, I'm shocked into silence. My mother used her eggs. A few warm tears fall from my eyes. At this moment I feel untethered from everyone in my family. Like I could ride away and never come back. My mother used her eggs. The sentence runs through my head, and I finally force it out.

"My mom used your eggs. You're Jay's biological mother."

I want her to laugh at me, hug me, and say, *Is that what you thought? No, that's not it,* but she looks at me in shock, on the verge of explosive anger or explosive weeping.

"You got it," she says. "My skinny, pot-infused egg. And Jay is gorgeous. Healthy as a goddamn stallion."

And now their rift, our distance, everything makes sense. I can't believe my mom told us such lies about Nicole. And our dad's a liar, too. Lied to us. Lied to everyone. Something in me comes to a boil. Everything buried deep rises, rises, rises, and the lights ahead are blinking, blinking, blinking.

I get off and run, recovering the terrain we just covered. I don't know where I'm going. I just go, every now and then looking at my phone. Finally, he answers:

At bar. Maggie Pond.

20

The rink is situated in the middle of hotels. Mist rises off of it. I don't know where he is, and part of me is tempted to get out on the ice and skate this adrenaline out. God, I spent so much time skating. Do I miss the feeling of my ponytail whipping through space, the edges of my skates glinting dangerously, ice shavings trailing behind me like mist? Not really. Though the thought of going back to school with family drama and an identity not based on skating feels horrible. It's something I'm known for, something I can always use as a reason or an excuse.

There are kids out there with their parents, smiling, laughing, something I never did on the ice even at their age, a miniature of myself, circling Coach, who'd stand in the middle like a horse trainer. I had loved skating backward, still do, I guess; it's the only time in life when going determinedly back is considered skillful and elegant. There is nothing elegant about what happened tonight. Nicole took me back, revealed the truth, and I've totally lost my balance.

"What's up?"

I turn to see him, and even though I'm in anguish, the sight of him brings relief. That is, until I register his coldness. It's like being with Nat again the day after. It's happening again with someone I didn't think it would happen with. Or am I being too needy?

"Thanks for meeting me," I say. "I don't even know where to begin. Nicole—"

"Your aunt?" he says.

"Yes." It's then I realize he must be irritated that he didn't know Skip and Nicole were my aunt and uncle—how, though unintentionally, I got him in trouble, maybe even put his job in jeopardy.

"Look, they'll be okay. I talked to Skip. He's not going to fire you or anything."

"Oh, thanks," he says, looking behind me, as if I'm wasting his time. "Thanks for saving my job."

I reach for his hand. "I'm sorry," I say. "Really, I am. I didn't mean to trick you or anything. I thought you knew. But listen. This is, like, crazy, life-altering stuff. I found out Nicole is Jay's biological mother! Jay—my brother. You met him, um, last night." I feel warmth at the thought of us in bed together, and how awesome it is to have the memory, a distraction, and to have Brose, who helps dull the edges of this blow tonight, this humiliation.

He looks down, removes his hand from mine.

"That's crazy," he says.

"I know," I say, already feeling relief. The music from the rink, the children's laughter. My boyfriend? Is that what he is, what he'll be? I'll have someone to accompany me through this.

"I don't even know what I'm going to say to my mom." I shake my head.

"Your mom," he says. "Skip's sister?"

"What? No."

"Skip's brother's wife, then?"

It's then I realize he still thinks I'm actually Annie Town.

"No," I say. "God, that would be complicated. No, Nicole's my mom's sister."

He puts his hands in his pockets, clenches his jaw. "So your last name is . . ."

"Tripp," I say.

"Tripp," he says. "Annie Tripp."

"That's me!" I exhale, and come into something that feels like peace—a kind of light-headed dumbness. A blackout. My mind must be up to something—gathering, locking pieces, but it's not getting back to me. I'm on the ice, gliding, floating.

"Well," he says, his tone shaking me out of my comfortable trance. "Good luck with your drama. Sounds like quite the soap opera."

He looks me over. It feels like a look he first gave me—judgmental. Thinking I was someone I was. His eyes are mean, a little glassy. He's been drinking, and I'm about to speak, but I can tell, right now, he's not there. He's not available.

He turns and walks away from me.

I am alone.

21

When I get home from the rink, I want to collapse into hibernation, but Jay's door is open. I take a breath and look in. How do I unleash this information that's making my body hurt? How do I tell him that everything he knows to be true is wrong? I can barely understand it myself.

"Out partying again?" he asks. He's lying on his back and tossing a ball into the air.

I start to speak, but stumble over my thoughts. I zoom into his eyebrows, his nose, seeing someone new, someone not entirely my brother, and yet feeling closer to him, more protective of him than ever. He doesn't know his deeper link to Nicole; he doesn't know what she's given our mother. He doesn't know his own story. Neither of us does. The scribbles that make us feel wiped out. I can't be here.

"You okay?" he asks, clutching the ball and sitting up. I feel so powerful, so in charge, and until now, I didn't realize that this isn't always a good thing to be. I could change his life in an instant.

"I'm . . . I'm whatever," I say. "I don't know what I am." My sadness and confusion morph into an even bigger feeling than anger. What else haven't our parents told us? Why don't they feel we deserve to be let in? Why aren't we collaborators? Why is our whole life a lie?

"God fucking damn it," I say.

"Whoa," he says.

My brother, I keep thinking. *You are my brother,* and I paid enough attention in biology to know that half of his genes are Nicole's.

He picks up his guitar. "I'll lull you," he says, and I'm glad he's playing so that he doesn't notice me studying his face. His brown hair, the tiny fan at the end of his left eyebrow, the roundness of his face, unlike the triangular shape of my mom's. Maybe his singing voice, too. No one in my family but Jay can keep a tune.

"Where were you tonight?" he asks.

I shake myself out of my trance and tell him some of the truth.

"I was working, and then I ran into Nicole in the parking lot. She was looking for Skip, and she was totally drunk. I got her home in a horse-drawn carriage."

"No way," he says, his green eyes lighting up. "She cracks me up." A smile stays on his face, thinking of his aunt Nicole, thinking of his biological mother, and it makes me feel so sick. I hear voices in the other room.

"Is Skip home?" I ask.

"Yeah. I guess he had a long night. He had to talk to . . . well, you know."

"What? Who?"

"Your Brose friend. And I guess he left his phone at the

restaurant, so he wanted to go to his room to decompress before he felt the wrath of his wife."

The wrath of Nicole. The wrath of Annie. My hands are in fists, and I don't know if I should scream or sob. I go to his bed to sit, so exhausted, so gutted. What did Skip say to Brose? Is that why he was so cold to me? Is it more than a Romeo and Juliet joke? Are we banned from one another? And yet this is another issue, one that's being pressed down by the one in my fists.

"Has Mom ever told you why she isn't close to Nicole?" I ask with my eyes closed. "Why we've never really seen them before?"

"She's just said that Nicole has issues."

I shake my head.

"But she seems fine to me," Jay says. "I mean, she's a little nuts, but not in a bad way. Maybe it's just petty sister stuff. Sibling stuff. Glad we're not that way." He punches my shoulder to roughen up his kind words.

"Maggot," I force myself to say, trying to attempt normalcy, clarity.

"I'm glad we're getting to know them." He starts to play "Wild Mountain Thyme," and I hold back tears. I can't help but feel the same way: glad to know them, but the gladness makes it hurt even more. They're all liars. Everyone I've ever depended on, and in Skip and Nicole's case, have grown to like, maybe even love, has lied. Everyone's a fraud, everyone's out to hurt and to fend for themselves. Everyone but my brother. Though even he's changed. It's like a part of him is gone. The mischievous glint in his eyes, the way all of his words would carry a lilt of sass. It's like he's grown up overnight.

I keep my eyes closed, listening to the song, feeling like it's my soundtrack on this wild mountain, but it conjures up too many emotions. I go to my room, erupting, my pillow hiding the sound of my punches and cries.

22

We move trancelike through our morning routine. Skip and Nicole know our patterns now. They'll give us vitamins after we finish our cereal. They'll ask us to put our bowls in the dishwasher, even though they don't need to ask anymore. Nicole has been quiet all morning. I keep shifting my eyes between her and Jay, and she doesn't even look at him, as if afraid any look will reveal everything. Secrets are the heaviest of weights. I imagine them making our bodies ache from carrying them for so long.

"You guys are quiet," Skip says. He sits at the counter, eating a bowl of oatmeal.

Jay and I sit alongside him, and we both emit primitive sounds, showing him we heard.

"Tired?" he asks. "Or—"

"Tired," we both say.

"Maybe you should go for a run," Nicole says, and sort of smiles in my direction. We have a private joke. A private drama as well. I can't carry it all. I need to get rid of these heavyweights.

"Am I still grounded?" I ask.

"Well, you're not technically grounded grounded," Skip says.

He gets up and rinses his bowl, then turns his back and makes a bunch of noise with the dishes.

"So I'm not grounded, but Brose isn't allowed to talk or be nice to me anymore?" I ask, and the kitchen noise stops, then slowly starts again.

"I'm going to ride before it gets crowded," Jay says, glancing at me.

"Skip?" I ask.

Nicole clears her throat. "Annie—why don't you come with me to work—"

"No," Skip says. "I can answer her."

"Okay," she says. "I need to go, but, Annie, would you want to take the shuttle up? Bring me my clothes? I'd like to talk to you too."

"Do I have a choice?" I ask.

"Yes," she says. "You do. I'll take you to the spa after. Then you can head to Steak and Rib?"

She's finding an excuse to be with me. The truth has been set free, and now we need to figure out what to do with it.

"Sure," I say, and I can tell this brings her relief. When Skip turns back around, there's a faint smile on his face, as if he and Nicole are finally figuring things out, and I wonder if he's right or completely deluded.

But the smile fades when she puts on her headphones and heads out the door. It's his turn to handle the truth, to figure out how to package and deliver it to me.

"I heard you talked to him last night," I say. "Which sort of explains—and sort of doesn't—why he was so rude to me. Is he not allowed to talk to me?" I laugh and shake my head. It sounds so ridiculous.

"He asked to talk to me," Skip says. "And no, I didn't tell him not to talk to you. I encouraged him to see you—to treat you the same way."

The same way. After getting caught on top of me. I want to return the truth. Hide in shame.

"Look," he says. He puts his hands on the counter, looks me in the eye. "Here's what's what. Brose's father is a good friend of mine. He used to live here. We were roommates. He moved to Denver but kept his condo here. I've known Brose his whole life. He started working here in the summer three years ago. Long story short: His dad was the contractor for the Aria residences. Desjarlais Construction."

My organs seem to plummet. What happens in our bodies that gives us this plummeting feeling? I look at my bowl of cereal, the soggy squares floating.

"Desjarlais Construction," I repeat, in a trance.

"His dad doesn't know he left school. You know that already. I did him a favor—hired him a few weeks before we found out you guys were coming. I suggested you take my name, just so there was no need to . . . just so you could be yourselves."

"Why didn't you tell me?" I ask, then don't even need to know the answer. Why would he? He didn't know I was with Brose. I hardly knew myself. And when he did find us naked—good god—his anger was probably doubled by having caught us because then he was forced to tell Brose who I really was.

"So you told him the truth?"

Skip looks down. "No. He came to me, and he knew."

Because he knew *me*. All along. Not that I'm Annie Tripp, but that I'm Annie: the spoiled girl slumming it in the kitchen before washing up and lounging back into life. And that was just the generous assessment. Now he has added to my résumé: daughter of a fraud, a con man who stiffed his dad and made him drop out of school to work in a kitchen, all because of my family's mistakes.

I put my head in my hands, mourning not only this sad summary, but his trust in me, the way he looked at me, even from the start, with judgment, sure, but like he always expected more. I mourn the moment we had the other night—how pure and sweet, no matter how brief—and how I thought it was just the beginning of something good and different and, well, real.

"What did he say?" I ask, keeping my head down. Tears slide. I flick them into my bowl.

"Not a whole lot," Skip says. "He just wanted to confirm what he knew to be true. And . . . he wanted to make sure he still had a job."

Skip clears his throat. "And that you . . . didn't."

I look up. "Didn't have a job?"

"Yes," Skip says.

"And what did you say?"

He scratches his cheek. "I said we'd talk. That that wasn't the issue." He takes my bowl. "And I told him to remember what he told me the other night. When he didn't know. When he thought you were just . . . you."

I wipe my eyes, trying to think of what Brose had said in the hallway, how I had strained, but couldn't hear everything.

"He said you weren't like anyone he's met before. That with everything he's going through, you're like an . . . energy."

We look at one another, then away, both embarrassed by . . . by what? By the tenderness my uncle had to communicate? The beautiful, melting words? Or by him communicating that it's over.

"So am I going to work today?"

Skip breaks eye contact.

"He needs this job."

"So he'll be there?" I ask.

Skip nods, and I leave it there. He didn't tell me not to go.

23

I take the shuttle up Boreas Pass. The driver, according to the name tag on her shirt, is MANDY from TEXAS. I wonder how many idiots walk onto this bus and say, "Hey there, Mandy from Texas!" I would use a fake name. DORK from MY LOINS. That would shut everyone up.

I wonder what brought Mandy here. I've begun to look at everyone around me, realizing they all have a story. Like this guy across from me, rubbing his goggles so vigorously you'd think they had measles. The old man by himself, wearing a ski hat with a little ball on top, like an ice cream cone on his head. A group of boys walking down the sidewalk, laughing. One of them jumping up like he's shooting a basketball. The two women in the back of the bus, both showing each other something on their phones and laughing. They could be longtime friends like me and Cee, or they could have just met like Rickie and me. The sky has cleared up, and the sun shines through the window onto my head. My hair seems to absorb all of it. I feel so close to the sun, like Icarus. He was unable to find that balance, as Mr. Earle had told us, "between arrogance and humility."

We seem to pass the same store over and over again. Stores filled with things you'd put on a shelf to die. On vacation, people will buy things they'd never buy in ordinary life. A nightgown with a moose on it? Sure! A box of fudge? Of course!

And then we turn off Main Street and head up the mountain, close to the sun. At the lodge I get out, nodding good-bye to Mandy from Texas.

Everyone greets me when I walk in, because that's what they're trained to do, I suppose. I'll never get used to someone opening a door for me, no matter how many times it's happened. At places with valets, I always rush to open my door before someone can open it for me, and now I rush past check-in just in case that goony guy is there, but then I slow down, look up, confident, feeling like I'm taken. Whether Brose wants me or not, I'm not available to anyone but him. I'm Annie from nowhere, Annie-maybe-Tripp, Annie-maybe-Town. Annie, the Tripp-Town kid. The anonymity, the duality, is empowering.

"Hey," I say to Nicole from the doorway. I walk in and put her clothes on the desk.

"Thanks," she says. "I'll change after our massages. I booked us for"—she looks at her phone—"nine thirty. Sit for a second."

I sit on the brown leather chair, feeling like I'm at Take Your Daughter to Work Day. I look out the picture window at the mountain, scarred with ski runs. It's like a huge hoopskirt.

"So," she says. "That was kind of a big deal last night."

The revelation about my mom, and now this morning, about Brose's dad. Big deals all right.

"Sure was," I say.

"Are you okay?"

I realize I'm staring at her face and thinking of all the similarities we share—our tone, our humor, our special social needs. We're so different, but there's this core similarity that seems glaring right now.

She's fiddling with something, and I realize it's one of those balls people use to help with stress. In middle school I had one, as well as a fidget cushion I could wiggle on and rubber bands around the legs of my chair I could kick. I supposedly had ADHD, and these were my "supports." I think I was just anxious, dreading practice, then getting home late and falling behind on homework, feeling dumb, tired.

"How are you doing with it all . . . I mean—" She blows on whatever's in her mug.

"Well," I say, "you're Jay's mom, and he doesn't know. My parents have lied to us our entire lives. I'm not doing too well. And to top that off, the guy I really like just so happens to have been screwed over by my dad. Which would normally be the biggest deal, but you being Jay's mom kind of blows it out of the water to frickin' . . . Siberia. I'm not well."

She nods, taking it all in. "Okay," she says, and seems to be organizing, rating the problems in front of her from Ten to One, Ten being the top priority. "About Jay," she says. "You can't think of it that way. Of me being his mom."

I look longingly at her ball. "I can't help it," I say.

"Sure you can," she says. "Just don't. I'm an egg donor, really. An anonymous donor. Your mom is Mom. It's simple. Like lending a neighbor sugar so she can make a cake."

"But you didn't just lend sugar. You lent her everything to bake the whole damn cake. And you're not a neighbor. You're not anonymous. You're her sister."

"Well, but with the cake analogy, half of the ingredients were from your dad—"

"And none were from my mom."

She looks at me over the rim of her mug. "Okay, let's just drop the cake. The point is that I'm not Jay's mother. It's like if your mom needed a kidney and I gave her mine."

"And that you're Jay's biological mother," I say, "who also gave my mom a kidney."

"Oh, Jesus," she sighs.

I raise my eyebrows, like, *Sorry, but facts are facts.* And then I bring up something that's been nagging me. It came to me late last night, on the cusp of sleep, and once it lodged into my head, I was upright and tormented. It drove me to the computer, where I researched people who donate their eggs. I learned they have to do these treatments to get their systems aligned or something, then get shot up with hormones, then it doesn't work and they have to get more eggs. A donor can give the eggs, and the receiver can use some or preserve them, too, for the future. Because sometimes it doesn't work. Or you want another baby.

When I came across this idea of egg preservation, I felt pinned back, like I was in a race car. My thoughts got stuck on replay. *For future, for future, I came so soon after, for future, for future use.*

I take a deep breath. "My mom used your eggs just for Jay?" I ask.

"What do you mean?" Nicole pulls on her earlobe. I don't break eye contact.

"She used your egg for Jay," I say. "Then had me naturally, right?" I look down at my hands, then back up. "You said you gave her *an* egg, but don't they take a *bunch* of eggs?"

She blinks, looks away. It's odd to think of us as these eggs, weird to think of the possibility of me frozen, lying in wait, not housed by anyone. I need to know. My leg shakes up and down as it often does when I take exams. Her stress ball is nearly flat, and then she releases it, and her shoulders move down, her face softens.

"Yes, they do that," she says. "They preserve the eggs. But your mom never told me she used any more." Her jaw clenches.

"And do you think that she didn't? After I came so soon after, so easily?"

Nicole sighs and blinks slowly as if I'm bringing something up that she herself had put to rest. "I choose to believe that, yes."

I don't believe this at all. Nicole may have chosen to trust my mom, but she must have had doubts. How did she get rid of these doubts? How do you ever? I think about my father, about Brose and his preconceptions of me. Even if or when you're cleared or forgiven, how do you abandon your misgivings? Is it just a matter of choice?

"Do you still believe in your choice?" I ask. "Your choice to believe her?"

We stare at one another, unblinking, as if in a duel.

"We've never talked about it," she says, which isn't an answer.

"That's convenient," I say. "That's why she shut you out, isn't it? She felt guilty or was afraid you'd want him back. Us back."

I look down, perplexed, lost, unhoused.

"I don't feel comfortable talking about this with you," she says.

"I don't feel comfortable either," I say, looking her in the eye until she looks away. "Too late. So did you?" I ask. "Did you want him back?" I need to say "him," not "us." I can't bear to say "us."

"No," she says, and looks up, places the ball on the desk. "No," she says again. "During the whole donation process, there's all this talk, this pep and prep talk—that I can't bond too much with the baby, that I can't feel entitled to him or judge the way your mom raises him. But I never felt those things. Ever. I looked at the eggs as something I wasn't going to use anyway. I didn't want him. Never even crossed my mind. He wasn't mine."

She hesitates and swallows. "And I never questioned how she got pregnant with you because I was afraid of her answer."

"That I'm from you, too?"

"Yes, but no." She looks at me like I failed something so simple. "I was afraid of the possibility that she didn't tell me." Nicole absentmindedly rolls the ball on her desk. "It started out okay. I came over all the time, helped out. I helped even more with Jay after you were born. Jay got attached. He was attached to other people, too, like your maid, but it was me she couldn't deal with."

"Sad," I say, imagining their bond and my mom's jealousy. She's a jealous person. I've never thought about this before, but with friends she seems to need to make them uncomfortable with themselves. I remember going to her friend Tara's house, how proud Tara was of her remodeled kitchen.

"Dark cabinets," my mom said. "Interesting." I watched Tara's face fall.

"My mom likes light," I said, and now I recall that I did this a lot that day, covered her unnecessarily mean tracks, not because I was some crazy nice kid, but because Tara's face made me sad. Our house was way nicer than Tara Laughlin's, so why make her feel bad about something she was so proud of?

"It is sad," Nicole says. "I was cut off. And I didn't do anything wrong. Not that I was pining away to spend every minute with you guys," she says, back to really squeezing that ball again. "I mean I had my own life, you know, *smoking pot*, but I didn't get to know you, and what's his name—Sammy—who is that kid? I don't know him at all."

She smiles, but I can tell she's doing it so I don't feel sorry for her, which I do. I think about that crib and Skip sanding the wood, putting it together, then having the confidence to put his child inside of it. Then I think about Sammy, how long my mom spent trying for him, as long as I remember, and I wonder if her efforts, the drugs, the hormones, the rounds of IVF, if they were all done to have one of her own. A real one, untainted by Nicole. I've never been a real one. Is that it? Something I've always felt finally has a name, and I don't know if it makes me sad or not. I kind of like the sadness, the idea of not belonging to my mom. Then the sadness does something strange. It turns into hope. Maybe I'm not hers, this person who has lied to me, this person who has tried to sculpt me into something stiff, this person who can be so cruel. What if Nicole is my mom? I could divorce my parents, hide out for life, never have to be associated with their mistakes, their selfish choices. Nicole can be my mom.

"I want to take a test," I say.

"Oh god," she says. "No." She searches my face, and I stare into eyes that look a little like my own.

"I didn't need to know," she says, and it takes me a moment to understand. She didn't need to know if my mom used her eggs because she gave them to her in the first place. "Why do you?"

Snow drifts across the window, and I can hear the sound of the wind in the trees.

I keep my gaze on the window. Part of me feels the same as Nicole right now—I don't want to know, not because I fear the answer, but I fear the lie.

"Because I want to know," I say. "It matters." I feel like I already know. I know by looking at her. I know by knowing her.

"Oh god," she cries, and puts her head in her hands. "How did this even happen? I shouldn't have children. I am so bad at this. I curse, I really do drink a lot. That's how this happened. Your mom is right about everything. I'm a disaster."

I hesitate before reaching over and quickly touching her hand on the desk. "You're not a disaster," I say. "You're learning. You've been really good with us," I force myself to say, but then I think, *She has been.* I've shared more with her than I ever have with my mother. The realization strikes me like a hot slap.

"Are you going to tell Jay?" she asks.

This is what bothers me the most. I can adapt to the knowledge of her being his biological mother, our biological mother, but I won't ever get used to him not knowing, of keeping something from him.

"I want to," I say, "but maybe you should."

"I can't be the one to tell him." She shakes her head, wipes her eyes. "Your mom should. If she could just come clean. About this . . . about everything."

"I had sex for the first time those two nights ago," I say.

I swear I hear her gulp.

"We used a condom," I add.

"Shit," she says, and looks down at her papers as if she made a clerical error. She sighs, then says words that don't form a sentence: "I don't . . ." and "You shouldn't . . ." and "We need . . ." Finally she says, "Well, how was it?"

I look outside, feel like I'm watching the beginning of a movie—the setup, the backdrop.

"It was a little scary," I say, "then strange, like this foreign object was filling me up . . . um . . . then it was okay . . . then good, and then Jay walked in."

She makes the most comical face, like she was eating a hamburger and it turned into a sundae mid-chew. Like, *What just happened to my food?* And, *Oh well.*

"And now," I say, "he won't even talk to me. Once again, my parents—the cause of everything."

We both nod, dumbstruck at the varieties of topics before us and wanting to move on. I don't know why I even said it. Why I said anything.

"Hey," she says. "Just be . . . be with it. Sorry, that doesn't make sense."

It sort of does. Because I don't really know anything about anything. My body seems to know some things, but my mind doesn't have the words for them yet. May as well go with it. Be with it.

"Please don't tell my mom," I say, feeling like a hypocrite—

keeping secrets. But sometimes people have to earn your secrets, right? She most definitely has not. "I won't fuck with you anymore," I say.

"Don't swear," she says, and rubs the inner corners of her eyes. "And don't worry—not my story to tell." She looks up. "Thanks for telling me."

"You too," I say, and then she takes an inhalation, like she's getting back to business.

"I wouldn't take a DNA test," she says. "Do you really need to know?"

Yes! I almost yell. What else is there to know?

"Yes," I say. "I really do."

"Then maybe you should just ask your mom," she says, so softly, yet the words ring clear. It's an easy solution that sounds so hard.

24

There's a big dent in the middle of my forehead from the massage bed. On the bus—driven by CODY from UTAH—I try to massage it out. Oh, the irony—massaging the massage. I feel good, despite it all, simultaneously relaxed and energized. I have a nervous excitement to go to work, like I'm carrying a new, curious weight, not so much a burden but a reminder, a good pressure. Though I should dread seeing Brose, I feel up to the challenge of pleading my case.

I get off of the shuttle a block early so I can walk a bit, get used to my rubbed-down body, and prepare my defense. I tiptoe through the mud in the parking lot, then enter through the kitchen. Brose is already here, taking the stems off of mushrooms. He looks up, not just surprised to see me but sickened by my presence. He snarls, it seems, shakes his head, disgusted and resigned—*Of course she's here,* he seems to be thinking. *She can do whatever she wants.* My confidence in my justifications and arguments weakens. They get tossed like the stems of those mushrooms.

I go to the sink to wash my hands, then walk over.

"Hey," I say, sidling up to him. I put on gloves, start to help. He's got his legs far apart so he doesn't have to hunch down to the table. He seems cleaner, like he just got out of the shower. His hair is brushed back, and he smells like laundry detergent.

Despite his coldness, a part of me gets warm, stirred. We still had that moment. That can't unhappen. It's strange that I didn't notice how handsome he was as soon as I saw him, how some things take time to announce themselves, how at first I only noticed Nat, the sleek-looking boy, the snake. The kind of boy my parents would like.

"I thought you weren't going to work here anymore," he says.

"I start school in a few days. I'll be gone soon."

Saying this out loud stuns me. I can't believe it has come so soon. When I first got here, I counted down the days, and now I'm dreading each passing one. I can't imagine seeing everyone in my town, at my school. The shame I'll feel if my dad's found guilty. The Ice Queen returns as a pathetic puddle. And if he's not guilty? I'll still know he is. I'll still carry the lies, the doubt, and what will our lives look like? How will I define myself? Defend myself?

"I'm dreading it," I say, wanting to say more, to be able to talk to him fully.

He stops working. "Yeah?" he says, his voice full of venom. "Tough life?"

"Well, yeah, actually. It is."

He scoffs, gets back to work, and I do, too, matching his angry, quick rhythm. He doesn't own tough times. I look around the kitchen, but no one else notices the tension. There are four others here, all nodding their heads to the music.

We continue to work in silence, stuffing the crab into the mushroom caps, his rough big hands, my smooth small hands. I don't know why, but I start to laugh, and when I look up, he has his lips tucked in, as if holding back a smile (or is that wishful thinking?), then he walks away, toward the stockroom.

I pull myself together and follow, find him sitting on a crate with his head in his hands.

"Sorry," I say. "I don't know what got into me. Nothing's funny."

"I disagree," he says.

"How so?"

"No matter what, every day, there's something. Something absurd. Something funny."

"True," I say. I look over at him, zero in on a freckle on his neck. "A lot has happened in two days."

"Yeah?" he says. His voice is so deep. I think of a cave and want to crawl in.

"Yeah."

I think of the points I had numbered in my head:

1. My dad hasn't been proven guilty.
2. He never intended to stiff his contractor.
   That was the market.
3. I never lied to you. I didn't know.
4. He has nothing to do with me. I'm still the same.
5. You've been judging me since we met.

But all of this, too, gets tossed.

"I'm so sorry," I say. "Whatever you're feeling toward me, I deserve. My dad . . ." Tears come to my eyes, and I brush them away like they're inconvenient pests. "It started out with bad luck, bad timing." I notice his irritation.

"Bad luck?" He looks up.

"Bad luck led him to make mistakes. I don't know everything, but I know I'd hate me too if I were you. I'd hate him, and I do sometimes." The words break me, the admittance of feeling the hate, but still not completely. He's my father. I can love him, too, right? I don't even care what I look like right now. I sob, and it's ugly, and for all I know, Brose has left, but then I feel his hands on my shoulders moving me, then pushing me down to sit on the crate he was using. My hands cover my face. His hand stays on my back, and I wish it could stay there forever, that good pressure.

"I meant to comfort you," I say. "Not the other way around."

I feel his hand lift. He sits on the floor in front of me, moves my hands from my face. God, his face, his eyes. They're like a sanctuary. I want nothing more than to go back to that night, erase my history, start there and repeat, repeat, repeat.

He leans forward, holds the back of my head, and kisses me. I feel a tear drop onto the top of my lip. He can probably taste the salt of me. When he pulls away, I feel reset, restored.

"I should get back," he says. "Then we'll . . . figure it out."

"Thank you," I say. "Can I stay?" I'm embarrassed by my voice, how desperate it sounds, but I really do want to work. I love the zone it puts me in. I love the camaraderie and also the fact that I have a job, that I can take care of myself.

"Yes," he says, and seems a little embarrassed, too. He pulls me up. I try to get a look at myself in the reflection of the fridge, but it's blurry.

"Hey, you know this fridge?" I say, knocking on it. "Skip and Nicole had sex in it."

He laughs. "Are you serious?"

"Yeah, when they were kids like us."

We stand, facing one another. Kids like us.

"That's funny," he says. "But ouch. Kind of cold."

We both look down and then he walks back toward the kitchen.

We go to our places at the counter, straighten out, get back to work, but now it seems like we have a good secret. I'm enjoying the restraint, like how things are so much funnier when you're not supposed to laugh.

The music is louder, and there are more people here. I feel like I've come out of hiding.

25

The night was smooth and fast, moved at a satisfying clip. I got to stay on the line since Forest could only manage doing dishes. Supposedly he "overate" a potent pot brownie. There was only one complaint of overcooked meat, but Freddie always takes the blame for that, only gets annoyed when people want it that way.

When we're done, I ask Brose if we can continue to figure things out, and he smiles, nods. We get our things and walk out into the cold night, a blue glow on the mountain.

"You sure Skip said it's okay to come out?" he asks.

"For some reason he trusts you."

"That's crazy," he says.

"So what are we going to do?"

"I don't know," he says. "I don't really feel like going out."

"Me neither."

I open the door of his truck. Inside it smells of dirt and leather. When he starts the engine, it rattles not quite to life, but more like to a half life. If this was Jay's truck and our lives hadn't changed, he'd simply get a new one. I guess I always thought it was those other girls who were materialistic—the girls in my grade who drive Range Rovers, who Instagram pics of themselves in front of a private jet—but I'm just as bad. I've never paid attention to how much something was. Even though I hadn't earned anything (until now), I felt entitled to whatever I had.

He blows into his hands and revs the gas, then turns the heat on high.

"We could go to my place," he says. "Talk."

"Talk?"

He looks at me, his brow furrowed, and I realize I have no right to be at ease yet. Things have forever changed.

"Look," he says. "About the other night. That was fast. I know you're leaving soon, and—"

He can't imagine how relieved I am. That my first time didn't end in a nod and an insult.

"It was perfect," I say. "My first time and all."

"Shit," he says. "I mean, I kind of knew once we started, but . . . I feel like an asshole, and then after, the way—"

"It's okay," I say. "It was a teachable moment."

We both smile like crazy.

"No, seriously," I say. "I'm happy. I mean, what followed wasn't ideal—my brother, Skip, you hating me . . . that wasn't too fun."

He doesn't answer.

"I know we're not . . . all good yet," I say. "I don't mean to sound like everything's fine."

He faces forward, nods his head, as if mulling it over. "I just meant, we can take it easy, talk. I should probably take you on a date before . . . next time, not that there will be a next . . . anyway. My place. Talk. Hang. Very innocent."

He reverses, which is a process. You'd have to be strong to use the shift and even turn the wheel. We chug inelegantly out of the lot.

"And we're off," he says.

I rub my thighs. "Like a herd of turtles."

"A dying breed," he says.

"Turtles?"

"No." He palms the lever. "Stick shifts."

"I've never even seen one before," I say.

We drive up Overlook, and I look at the town below, a small space of light surrounded by darkness. I text Nicole to let her know where I am and then think it strange that my mom doesn't know. I'm on a mountain with a boy. A mountain man. I'm riding in a truck. Do you know where your daughter is? Do you know *who* she is?

He turns the radio up, and the music is like a heavy scarf. This night of stars and wood smoke. This is perfection. Nothing is flawless, but everything is moving toward its mysterious conclusion. I want to put blinders on like the horse so I don't have to see the stimulation of my life. I can just feel safe and calm in these imperfect moments. He shifts, and then we turn the corner into a condo development.

We get out, and walk up the snowy steps. He opens the door to a clean and pretty space. He turns on some lights, and I follow him toward the kitchen.

"When are you going to tell your dad you're not going back to school?" I ask.

He opens a drawer, pulls out two spoons. "When it's too late to do anything about it," he says. "I know it will be a relief for him not to pay, but he still won't like it."

I have no idea what kind of financial situation we're in or will be in. I don't even know what I'd prefer. I'd feel even worse if we weren't affected at all. If Cee and Brose and families from school were devastated, and we were just fine. I'm so angry at my parents for making us go back to face all of this and for not preparing us at all. What's our plan B? How will a bad verdict change our lives?

"Are you going to miss it?" I ask. "Did you like it there? Big party school." I make an attempt to lighten things up.

"I loved it," he says, which only darkens things. "Yeah, it was fun, like, socially, but I've kind of partied enough. I've gotten my sillies out."

"Your sillies out?"

"Yeah, didn't you do that in kindergarten?" He moves through the space at ease, opens the freezer, and gets out a gallon of ice cream while singing, "I'm going to shake, shake, shake my sillies out, clap, clap, clap my crazies out—you never did that?" He puts scoops of ice cream into two bowls.

I bite my lower lip and shake my head.

"Well, you missed out." He puts the spoons into the bowls, and I reach over for mine.

"Don't eat it yet," he says. "You're witnessing my nightly routine. Come." He takes his bowl and walks toward the sliding doors, then opens them. A blast of cold air shoots in.

"What are you doing?" I say. "It's snowing. And you have a fireplace." I hold up my bowl. "Cold." I tilt my head toward the fireplace. "And hot."

"I have a hot tub," he says, lifting his bowl. "Cold and hot. You don't mind getting in with your underwear, do you?" He looks back and crinkles his nose.

"Real innocent," I say.

"Our ice cream is now reaching the perfect texture," he says, taking off his sweater and then his pants. He keeps his boxers on.

"Um, I thought we were just talking."

"Your bra and underwear are the same as a bathing suit. Here. I'll turn around."

"It's okay," I say, then fully undress down to my bra and underwear. Thank god it's a decent set.

I notice myself, my breasts smallish but full, my torso long, lithe. I've always thought of my body as something to work, something to present versus use and enjoy.

I quickly get in with my ice cream, making a splash since I got in like a spaz. A stream of bubbles shoots into my lower back. This has to be the best feeling: the hot water like fire, cold air, cold ice, crowded stars above.

"This is awesome," I say.

"Right?"

He stands, and I realize that's probably the best way to do this so that the bowl doesn't rest in the water. I challenge myself to just stand up, and the air hits my chest, and the water slides down my body. "This is funny," I say.

"What's funny?" he says.

"Oh, you know, eating ice cream practically naked with you."

He smiles, but then I ruin it by saying, "Is this what you do with all the girls?" which makes him roll his eyes.

"Sorry," I say. "That was stupid."

"I didn't mean for this to be, like, sexy time," he says.

I hold my ground. "You wanted me in a hot tub mostly naked," I say.

"No. I just wanted to show you something nice."

I look down at his body under the water. He looks down, too. "That's not what I meant!"

I laugh. "I know, I know," I say. "This is really nice." I look up at the snow, falling so softly, then dissolving over our heads.

"Just ice cream," he says. "Just this."

I tilt my head back, making my hair wet and slick.

He's resting his head against the edge and looking up.

"When you first met me," I say, "why didn't you like me?"

He smiles. "I did. I just didn't want to. I felt I knew you. Girls like you." He laughs and looks over. "It's not like I'm from the hood or something. I went to Kent, lived in a nice house. My family did well. Just after . . . everything. Everything I knew was tainted."

I don't want the rest of my ice cream, feeling sick. I put it down.

"But I was wrong," he says. "You are what I thought, and you aren't. Who knows *what* you are. We're all lots of things."

"Deep," I say.

"Yeah, I'm in college."

I laugh, but what he says settles in an empty place that needed to be filled. I felt trapped by Cee's one definition of me, my school's, my parents' expectations of me, the ways I was supposed to act, the people and even sports I was supposed to like and dislike.

"Maybe that's true about my dad?" I say. "He might be lots of things, too. Not just the one."

"You mean, like, he's more than just that asshole who pulled a Ponzi scheme?"

I flinch, and Brose hits his head. "Sorry," he says, and even though I'm here, prepared to lie down in front of him, submit and admit and apologize, a part of me just can't give in, will probably always defend him.

"Yup," I say. "That asshole's my dad. That's him." I lift my arms. "So that's me."

He closes his eyes, then pushes up and moves in front of me. "Are you guys close?"

"I don't know," I say, realizing, or perhaps remembering, that my dad doesn't really know me very well.

"I can't imagine," he says, gone in his own thoughts. "You must feel . . ."

"Betrayed," I say. "Embarrassed. Guilty."

"You didn't do anything," he says.

"It's just how I feel," I say, and he looks down.

"And now you've got the whole Nicole-is-your-brother's-mother dilemma."

I bite my lip. "Can you believe it? You still think I'm the girl who has it all?"

He shakes his head. "See? We're many things."

We talk about the ways I could tell Jay, or if that's even my news to tell. I tell him my own DNA concerns, which opens up a whole new can of wtf's.

"This is good," he says, taking my hand and shaking it under water. "We're talking things out. Workshopping."

"Can we workshop you now?" I ask, and move toward him, putting my hands around his waist.

"Have at it," he says.

I lean in to kiss him, tasting the mint on his tongue. He tastes me back. We do this for what seems to be forever and then he pulls me to his lap.

"Getting my sillies out," I say.

He kisses my forehead, and I rest my head on his hot and cold shoulder.

He brings me home even though I wanted to stay, but it feels good to walk up to the front door, full of both satisfaction and longing. I open the door as quietly as I can, but see Skip and Nicole on the couch, his arm around her. They gaze at a fire. I immediately think of Brose, his arm around me, and envision them being versions of us, pretty much doing the same thing. I feel like we could all do this together—the four of us in the same room—and this gives me such a feeling of pride and adultness, or like the things I have done are okay and nothing to be ashamed of.

"Hi," I say, and close the door behind me.

Skip looks back. "Hey, kid," he says.

"We waited up for you," Nicole says.

"Am I in trouble?"

"No, you're not in trouble. Relax. We just waited."

"We like you," Skip says, and we all grin. I sit on the chair next to the couch.

"This is very romantic," I say.

"Your hair's wet," she says, and so I shut up.

Skip takes his arm off of Nicole and leans forward. "So, your mom called," he says, and I immediately think, *She's not my mom,* and then feel bad about thinking that and my instinct to immediately reject her. I don't know which scenario I'd prefer. Her lying to me and Nicole is my real mother. Or her not lying and Nicole is only Jay's real mother.

"Are we going home?" I ask.

"They're supposed to have the ruling in the next few days," Nicole says. "Could be as soon as tomorrow. But, yes, I'm sure you'll be home soon. You may commute the first few days of school, but . . . the call was just to check in."

"Jay said you paid a little visit to Ken Rush?" Skip says, leaning forward as if we're having a private meeting.

"Yeah," I say. It seems like that was a lifetime ago, but for Jay, I guess no other event pushed it aside. He didn't learn about his father's corruption, then go on to lose his virginity, start to really like someone, lose that someone because of his father's corruption, try to get that person back, which made him like that person even more, and he didn't find out his mom wasn't really his mom. Holy shit, how am I standing? Life came at me fast.

"I wanted to see my friend Cee," I say. "Who probably isn't my friend anymore."

"You found out some pretty hard things?" He raises his eyebrows.

"Just some things you guys and other people have probably known all along," I say, and by their guilty looks, I know I'm right. Everyone's known, and I was too naive to believe it.

"It's a lot to process," Skip says. "Big days ahead. They're hearing summaries today and then sentencing will follow."

"Did my mom want to talk to us, or did you ask her to?"

"She needs to talk to you," Nicole says, which doesn't answer the question. The heat of the fire feels good on my wet hair. A lot of hot and cold tonight.

"Yeah, I'd like to talk to her too," I say, and Nicole looks sharply at me.

"These next couple of days will be big," she says, as if what I have to say shouldn't come before that. My mom will have enough to deal with—her husband could go to jail, she will lose all of her friends, all of her comforts, and Nicole is asking me not to bring up the other issues, the ones that won't change because of a ruling. Though for me, the ruling won't change anything anyway. If he's guilty, he's guilty. If he's innocent, he's still guilty, and that will last forever. Still, Nicole is asking me to wait. She is, as always, thinking of her sister, and I can't help but admire her for it.

"I know," I say. "So now what?"

I don't know why I ask this. I'm not sure what I even mean by it or how it can possibly be answered.

Now what?

He loses and we lose everything?

He wins and we go back? Continue on?

Does he learn his lesson, or does he get away with it, earn more, spend more, need more, hurt more?

I remember when the units first went on the market, he told me things were going well. He told me this was so special. Every detail was considered, every corner, hinge. Materials from all over. German tile, Italian marble, the greater the distance, the more my eyes were supposed to widen.

So now what?

I think of Cee in Kansas, standing in a barren field. I think of the shop owner who spat out my last name, Joanie the secretary, Brose and his family, the countless strangers who've lost their savings, who've been abandoned, replaced, moved, forgotten. *Going well for who?*

I imagine him answering me, with no guilt whatsoever, "For us. For you."

I never questioned the things I've always had at my fingertips. I never thought that the way we got our things was at the expense of others, both loved ones and strangers.

"We wait," Nicole says, finally answering the question I never needed to be answered.

I say good night to my aunt and uncle, then go to my room and wait.

26

The next day, I wake up and wait. What else is there to do? I wait for my mom to call. I wait with my brother, watching *The Naked Spur* and *Tootsie*. I wait with Rickie, playing virtual golf and telling her everything over coffee at the Shack.

Now I wait with Brose in the Steak and Rib kitchen. Rickie has come in early just to hang out. I can feel them looking over my head, as if trying to silently agree upon what to talk about.

"It will all be okay," Brose says while we peel carrots.

"It will be okay if my dad goes to jail, or if we're broke?" I ask, and yet as soon as I say this, I look up at him and hold back. It's extremely awkward to vent to him, and I don't know how we're going to overcome this.

"Yes," he says. "Either. Both. It will be okay."

I should have left it alone. When he first said it would be okay, he was sincere; now he's bitter, resentful that it *could* be okay, and I have to let him be. Though does that mean I have to be okay with him not wanting the best for me?

"We'll all be okay," Rickie says. "What else is there to be?"

"That's the question," Brose says.

"I don't want to show my face in school," I say, scraping carrots furiously. They're both being like my brother—unrecruitable into my negative space. Though, I should say, that was the old version of Jay. He's a new person, too.

"Wear sunglasses," Brose says, and I know he's trying to cheer me up, and I know I need to let him. I'm working fast, my pile of shreds much bigger.

"You're supposed to peel, not whittle," Brose says.

"Fine."

We continue in silence.

"I'm going to go change," Rickie says, and walks toward the office nook. "You guys keep on keeping on."

"Sorry," I say. "I know it's hard to hear me complain. I'm just nervous."

"We can take turns," he says. "But I'll let you have the mic for a while."

I bump my hip into him as a thank-you. Nat walks in and smirks like we're something cute, something small, even though he looks so reduced in here, a preppy boy who couldn't cut it in the kitchen. While I don't want my problems, part of me likes the way they bring me up to this weird vantage point, making everything that was once big so tiny, a speck.

"Where is everyone?" Nat asks.

"Who's everyone?" I want to throw something at him. Maybe this pointy carrot.

Nat makes a sound like a cat scrapping, even though my voice was perfectly calm.

"Why'd you just do that?" I ask. "Why did you make that noise?"

He laughs. "Shit, relax." He looks around for assurance, for another laugh. So insecure. I can see everything from up here.

I feel Brose's leg press into mine. "I think she's pretty relaxed," he says, and Nat just shakes his head with an embarrassed smile on his face, then leaves.

"Do you need to cool off?" Brose asks. "'Cause we can go to the walk-in."

I laugh—something I haven't done in days, it seems—and he gives me a new carrot.

And so I wait, peeling carrots.

Later, I wait in the hot tub with him and a bowl of mint ice cream. I wait for him to kiss me, but he doesn't. I don't take offense. I can tell he's deep in his thoughts, and I let him rummage through them. But the more he rummages, the more distant he seems to get.

"You okay?" I finally ask.

"Yeah?" he says. "I think I need some time."

I leave, now waiting for him, too.

Later, I wait on the couch, this time with Skip and *The Searchers*, John Wayne in the wilderness of Texas, searching for his lost niece.

27

I wake up on the couch, disoriented, with a blanket over me. I sit up to face the kitchen, smelling dough and maple syrup.

"Morning!" Nicole yells.

"Oh my god," I say, and curl into a ball. "You're so perky."

"It's such a nice day," she says from the kitchen.

Her cheeks are flushed. She looks like a fitness instructor. Skip walks out from the hall, dressed for the mountain. He has goggles on his head. I grunt my hello.

"Any news?" I ask.

"Nope," Nicole says.

"What about when school starts?"

"You can commute," she says. "I mean, you start on a Wednesday. That's just three days until the weekend. I'm sure everything will be wrapped up by then."

She is being annoyingly chipper.

"And we thought we'd all go take some runs together," Skip says.

He's all casual, like this is any other day. I look back and forth between the two of them, understanding this is their plan, designed to take the child's mind off of things.

He sees my skepticism.

"Come on, Niece Annie," he says, running his hands through his hair, forgetting about his goggles, which fall to the floor.

"Uncle Klutz," I say, and he stands up, grinning, probably thrilled with my cheesy humor. There must be nothing worse to a man than a depressed teenage girl, not because he empathizes but because he feels inept.

Now Jay waltzes out, clearly already recruited, though he probably wasn't a hard sell. He looks at me, rolls his eyes, telling me to just go with it.

I stand up with the blanket wrapped around me and go to my room to change. I guess I wouldn't mind going fast down a hill. It actually sounds like a great idea.

We wait in the lift lines, we wait on the lift, but the waiting is good now. Being outside, feeling the sun and wind. We're high above the ground, Skip and I, on a two-seater, swinging slightly with our snowboards hanging. Life from this height is nice. The lift comes to a stop, and we swing between the rows of pines.

"I'm scared," I say to Skip, his big gloves on his legs. He lowers his sweatshirt so I can see his mouth.

"Of the lift?" he asks.

I shake my head.

"Of course you are," he says. "I am, too. For you. I don't want anything bad to happen to you. You know what's good about all of this? Not good, but just one positive thing?"

"What?" I say. Our shoulders touch.

"Getting to meet you guys. I know you didn't pick us to live with. I'm not an idiot. We were probably your parents' only option."

"The only ones my dad didn't screw over," I say.

"We were their easiest option. From us there'd be no questions asked."

The lift starts up again.

"Actually, Nicole had tons of questions," he says. "But we would never have said no. It's been great for us."

"Us, too," I say.

I hear the sounds of skiers and snowboarders below, swishing through the snow.

"Nicole told me everything," he says.

I'm not sure what he's referring to. That I had sex? Oh, god.

"She told me you know that she helped your mom out a long time ago."

"That's one way to put it," I say.

"Yeah," he says.

"Were you around then?" I ask.

He smiles to himself. "Yup."

"And you didn't have issues?"

"I'm the most issueless guy you'll ever know, but yes, I did." He pauses. "But there was no talking her out of it. Nicole was set on helping your mom."

"It's just so weird," I say. "It's crazy—I forget about it sometimes and then I remember, and I look at Jay and feel awful about not telling him. And then I get furious at them for keeping it from us. Keeping so much from us . . ."

"We've always thought if you keep it a secret, then it's something, well, secret, something to hide instead of take pride in. It's different, sure, but it's not shameful. Nicole always felt ashamed, but if it had never been a secret, then—no shame." He holds up his big gloved hands.

We're almost to the top. I swing my legs to get the blood flowing.

"Something to keep in mind," he says. "Secrets suck."

"How's the secret crib coming along?" I ask.

Skip laughs. "That's different. That's a surprise."

We glide up toward the end, over the tops of trees.

At the top, Jay is skating his board toward a group of people I recognize, and I feel like I'm in an elevator, my stomach dropping. I slide off the lift in their direction. There's Mackenzie and Bree, in matching white beanies. I recognize their laughter—not the sound, but the type—laughter to hide their embarrassment because they suck at snowboarding. Laughter because they're with boys. Laughter to show how much fun other people aren't having. I think I recognize Joffrey and Eric. Yes, those are Joffrey's thick brown curls, tumbling out of his beanie. He seesaws on his snowboard and pulls up his baggy pants. Eric's on telemark skis. He's easy to recognize with his orange hair and lanky, long body.

"Yo!" Jay calls. The boys turn.

"Dude," Joffrey says. "What's up?" Jay slaps hands with him. I catch up and stand by my brother. Eric doesn't have the same cocky ease he usually has and nods at us in an oddly formal way.

"Oh, hey," says Mackenzie, and she and Bree look me up and down. I feel like I'm going through security at the airport.

"What are you guys doing here?" my brother says. "You should have hit me up." Jay punches Joffrey in the shoulder. No one speaks. "What," Jay says. "You guys allowed to talk to me?"

"Yeah, we be classy," Joffrey says. "What's up, Annie?"

"Hey," I say.

"Heading to chair six if you guys want to cruise," Jay says. "We're with our aunt and uncle, though."

"Skip-Nic," I say. "Like picnic." They all look at me like I've blurted out *ball sac* or something.

"We were just going to the terrain park," Eric says. "Training for next weekend."

"That's right," Jay says. "Forgot it's being held here this year."

"Yeah," Eric says.

"Yeah," Jay says, eyeing Eric as if he can't see him well. I can tell he's thinking, *Is this friend gone?*

I look back for Skip and Nicole and see them by the lift, giving us distance. Nicole waves, and I lift my hand.

"So cute," Mackenzie says. "They're like your foster family."

Joffrey laughs. "Hope they don't mistreat you," he says.

"We occasionally get touched inappropriately," I say.

"It's not our fault," Jay says, and I feel a warmth. He has my back. We can look like weirdos together.

The girls look at us like our weirdness has tripled its strength, and it has. I glare back at them, thinking, *Fuck you, fuck you, fuck you.*

"Good running into you," Joffrey says, tilting his chin. He's trying so hard to put up a good front, and I can tell Jay appreciates it, like he's getting fired quietly and kindly. I try to communicate with Joffrey, too, with my look: *Thank you, thank you, thank you.*

"See you guys at school," Jay says, prompting Bree and Mackenzie to look at one another with alarm, like, *How dare we show our faces again?* They're going to have so much fun hating us.

"Let's roll," Eric says, which prompts me to roll my eyes.

This is what school will be like. Every damn day. Strip-searched and judged, loudly and quietly ridiculed. Infuriating those who've been affected by my dad and entertaining the remainders.

The girls push off, twittering like baby birds. Jay puts his hand out for the dude hand slap transition to half hug. Joffrey does the routine and then it's Eric's turn. Jay holds his hand out slightly to the side like he's swinging a racquet.

Eric just looks at him. "Sorry, man . . ." And then he leaves. He rolls.

"I'm not my father," Jay says, and then, when they've all left, he says in a funny and exaggerated serious voice, "I am not my father." He shakes his head. "Jesus. Anyway."

"He kind of sucked a ton," I say.

"Yeah, well, just protective of his dad, I guess. Same as us."

Same as us. I don't know how Brose can bear to be with me. I worry that he can't.

We're surrounded by peaks and valleys and a swath of white snow before us, billowing when the wind blows.

"Our lives are going to be squashed," I say.

"We'll be okay," he says. "We have each other."

I raise my eyebrow, suspicious of his sentimentality, but he looks distracted, caught in complex thought.

"If Dad goes to jail," he says, "it might be liberating for him, you know? To come to terms with it. Consequences, being alone, having time to reevaluate, start again."

"There is nothing liberating about being stabbed in jail," I say.

"Jesus, Annie, it's not that kind of jail."

"Who cares what kind! Did you see how your friends acted?"

"We'll get new ones," he says, and I sigh. It's like I've tricked myself into thinking I'm a different, better person, but when I was just confronted with our old life, I cowered. I don't want to self-reflect, reevaluate. I want what I've always had.

Nicole and Skip slide up to us with looks of concern.

"You good?" Skip asks.

"Great," Jay says.

"Who were those guys?" Nicole says.

"Friends," Jay says, looking at me. "From home."

She looks back and forth between the two of us.

"No one said or did anything to you, did they? Tell me the truth." She is strapped in, so she keeps flapping her arms for balance. "Tell me. I will wring their fucking necks, I swear to god."

"Jeez, OG," I say. "Nothing happened."

"What's OG?" she asks. "What happened?"

"Original Gangsta," Skip says, and Jay hides a smile.

"You need to let me know things," she says. "Especially with school starting. If there are bullies or people texting you, like, mean shit, I will waltz right into the principal's office. Teachers too! They can be self-righteous bastards."

Skip pats her shoulder. "It's okay, honey."

"It didn't look okay," she says. "You don't look happy." She leans on Skip and looks at Jay, something so fiery in her expression, like she's protecting him from imminent danger. She's a mother bear.

"I'm perfectly happy," Jay says. "Pitying glances—that's all we had to reckon with."

"Well, it's over now," she says. "I say we buck up and do a few more runs, go fast, feel the wind and the elements, clear our heads, then get a hot chocolate afterward. And one of those mammoth cookies?"

Skip grins and holds a thumb up behind her so she can't see. It's like a cue card telling us to laugh or applaud.

"Sounds great," Jay says with enthusiasm.

"Cookies," I say.

We take the gondola down to the lot. The collar of my sweater is crusted with ice. My chin is numb, my cheeks feel slapped, and it feels so good. I've forgotten how much I love this sport, this "ugly sport," as my mom would say.

Snowboarding boots are the only boots I'll put on from now on, so there's another thing that defines me erased. Gone. It's then that I wonder: Did my coach really quit me, or did we quit him? Is this another lie my mom told me? That I'm not good enough, when really, she couldn't afford him anymore? Or he just didn't want to be associated with our family. This is yet another thing I want to know that will hurt so much to know.

There are two other women skiers riding with us, and they look to be around eighty years old.

"So nice seeing a family together," one of them says. She has a pink suit on that looks like a giant puffy onesie. I want one badly.

She says something to her friend that makes her laugh and cover her mouth. She has strong cheekbones padded with soft-looking skin. You can tell they've been friends for a long time. There was a time when I was convinced Cee and I would be like them, outlasting whatever we ran into over the years, but now I know we've already morphed into someone unrecognizable to the other.

"When my son was your age, he wouldn't be caught dead skiing with me," one of the ladies says to Nicole.

Nicole laughs and begins to explain, placing her hand on Jay's leg. "Oh, no, he's my—"

"His loss," Jay says, tapping Nicole's boot with his. "Plus, my mom leaves me in the dust."

Nicole is caught off guard. She looks at me, almost shy, and I wonder what it felt like just then, that second, to be his mom, to hear him say *my mom*. She looks stunned, proud, aglow.

The ladies coo at Jay's sweetness, and Skip begins a round of small talk. Briefly, we learn about each other. They're friends who live in Arizona. We are the Town family who live in Breckenridge. The lie is like a bright truth.

Nicole goes into the lodge for the cookies, then distributes them into our eager hands. The chocolate chunks are as big as eyes. We eat as we walk, and I don't think I've ever seen people eat delicious cookies with such melancholy. We've come down, literally, from our high, no longer soaring over the trees or gliding down mountains. We're at street level, pushing on, our snowboards under our arms, walking into the wind to Skip's truck.

"That was nice," Skip says, trying to maintain our previous high, and it was, but now there's phone service. There's internet. I see Nicole check her phone.

"Nothing yet," she says.

Jay and I get in the back of the truck. My mom would be pissed if she saw us like this. Unsafe and trashy-looking in the back of a pickup. I love it. We keep our goggles on to block the wind. Skip makes his way out of the lot.

"Did it work?" I ask.

"Did what work?" Jay says.

"Skip-Nic's little outing to get our minds off of things."

"It worked for a while," he says.

We drive down Main Street, and the town looks peaceful in the late day, the sun a low blur. Everyone is heading somewhere—families, teenagers, maids in matching uniforms.

"You should check your phone," he says, but doesn't say anything when I don't answer. I don't want to check my phone.

"I looked up *bear garden*," Jay says. "It's from Henry the Eighth. A state of near chaos or turmoil, but back in the day, there were these actual bear gardens—people would gather around and watch blind bears get whipped until blood dripped down their backs."

"Are you kidding me?" I say.

"Life was brutal," Jay says. "People are brutal."

That actually makes me feel physically ill, and then I'm even more sick with myself for wanting to show Bree and Mackenzie anything at all. Then I'm just as petty as they are. I keep trying to convince myself I've changed, that I can go high, but screw it. I'm going to go back and forth—both striving and failing, seesawing between goodness and selfishness. I give up, which, oddly, feels like a gain.

I watch all the people around us on the street, each one having something they're struggling with, longing for, though at this moment, surrounded by this golden light, most of them are on vacation, off the tracks of their normal lives. If only life could always be off track.

"School's going to be brutal." I tilt my head back and look at the fan of clouds. "You think we'll be in a bear garden?"

"No blood," Jay says. "Maybe some sweat."

I feel good that we'll have each other. I'll snowboard, see Brose, if he'll have me. I'll study like crazy. I'll keep my head down, hide. I look up, trying to read my fortune in the sky.

"This show the other night reminded me of you," my brother says.

I look at him. "What?"

"This show," he says again, and there's that old glimmer in his eye that I haven't seen for a while. "I thought of you when I saw it. Did you ever see *I Didn't Know I Had an STD*?"

I bite my lip, shake my head. "I didn't see that one. But I saw one the other night, too, and it made me think of you."

"What a coincidence!"

"I know! So, have you ever see that show *I Didn't Know I Had a Half Peen*?"

"No, I regret that I have not, but have *you* seen *I Didn't Know I Was Pregnant with Triplets! I Just Thought I Was Frickin' Huge*?"

I give him a look. Joke failed.

"Or, um—" he says.

But I cut him off: "*I Didn't Know That a Disorder Was Named After Me?*"

"Or!" he says. "*I Used to Be an Ice Queen, but Now I'm a Dishwasher?*" His smile falls, but I'm not offended.

I laugh. "Or," I say, "*I Used to Have SO Many Friends, but Now My Dad Is a Crook.*"

"Ouch," he says. "Missed that one, but it's probably something I should see."

We look at one another, slight smiles, and then he sits back against the tailgate and I sit back against the window, hearing Nicole and Skip laughing about something.

We pull into our neighborhood.

I smell other people's dinners and am comforted by the thought of us all side by side, living. We slow down, and I take my goggles off, feeling the fresh minty air on my face. I text Brose, wondering where we stand. The ground always seems to be shifting.

"Oh my god," Jay says. "That's Mom and Dad."

I lean over and look at the driveway, and it takes a while for the image to reach my brain or something. It's just wrong— seeing them in this space—and I feel a bit guilty that this is my first thought. It's like when my mom would pick me up from school or sleepovers when I was little, and she'd be happy to see me and I'd feel bad that the sight of her disappointed me because I just wanted to stay. But then I think of everything— and it's a long list—and I don't feel guilty at all.

"Sammy," I say. "Look at him. He's bigger."

The truck comes to a hard stop, and we're all stunned into

stillness. Nicole and Skip sit there staring. Jay and I don't get out. The neighbor is in the process of deflating the Santa. I can hear the air sigh out, see the puff of red, white, and black slowly collapse.

We finally get out, and our family, the Tripp-Towns, meet again.

28

wkward hugs and hellos. Skip immediately says he'll throw some food together, and I help, needing to do something with my hands. This is just too weird for me. I can't even remember the last time I saw my mom and Nicole together. It's a memory that only exists in storage somewhere.

The question has already been asked—"How did it go today?"—and it has been answered by my father: "Good. But let's sit for a sec, huh?"

My mom and dad, sitting on the couch, keep looking over the place with small, timid smiles. I feel defensive, like these are my friends they're silently judging. And yet that was me just two weeks ago.

Jay is making a fire, and Nicole is tidying up, probably totally mortified that they're here and she didn't have time to stage the place. I feel bad for her, and oddly vigilant. My mom gets up, holding Sammy. She looks bewildered walking around, and I see things through her eyes, all our ski gear, the books and magazines, the knickknacks that would never be in our home, like the ceramic name tag she has picked up from a side table: HELLO MY NAME IS DOUCHEBAG. She sets it down, then wipes her hand on her pants. Sammy squirms in her arms, and she reluctantly puts him down on the carpet.

Nicole places a glass of red wine on the table in front of my mom, then sits in the chair across the room from her. My mom takes a sip and grimaces.

"We had fun today," Skip says. He's chopping zucchini, and I'm smashing garlic. "Up on the mountain."

My dad looks at my mom. He pats his neck with his hand-kerchief.

Just when I'm about to scream, *Cut the chitchat!* my dad says, "I've been sentenced to three years."

"Oh my god," Nicole says, and I just blink and blink, like there's something in my eye. No matter how much I've thought about it, I just didn't believe this could actually happen. I still don't really believe it—I'm convinced he'll be able to work something out like he always does.

"What are you going to do?" I blurt out.

Jay mutters, "Jesus." I don't think he realizes how much lighter fluid he's using. He's in a zoned-out state of pure anger.

"Buddy," Nicole says to him. "No need for an eternal flame."

My mom glances between the two of them.

"Were you thinking about us at all?" Jay says.

I could barely hear him. He throws a match in, and the fire jumps to life with a hollow, explosive sound.

Sammy crawls off his mat that my mom has needlessly laid down on the carpet, and he moves across the floor, then stops to watch the fire, banging his legs with his tiny fists.

"Today?" my dad asks. "Of course."

"Before today," Jay says, turning away from the fire and

facing my dad. "When you made decisions. Did you think about us going back to school with the people whose families you screwed over? I'm not going back there."

My dad has on that expression he gets when someone's challenging him—a flicker of annoyance in his eyes, amusement in his mouth. Jay has the same expression at times, but it never lasts. It surrenders into either embarrassment, empathy, or genuine anger. You can always see his true emotion. And now I see that Jay isn't as impenetrable and brave as I thought. He's just as embarrassed and afraid.

My dad leans forward, his elbows on his knees. "Of course I thought of you guys. I did this for all of you."

Sammy lets out a happy yell. He's on the other side of the living room now, near Nicole.

"Hey," she says. He looks up at her, gaping, then grabs her legs, using them to pull himself up. She looks down at him and waves.

I look over at Skip, his knife hovering over the vegetables.

"I was always thinking of you," my dad says.

"Then why did this start out so casually?" Jay says. "Why didn't you prepare us—"

"And what do you mean, you did this for us?" I ask. "Did what? Lie to people? Con people? So that—what? We could have *stuff*? *Things*?"

"Annie," my mom says.

"What?" I say. "How long have *you* known?"

"That's enough." My dad stands up. He looks like he did when he was giving the presentation at the launch years ago— at the helm, and like everyone below him better get up and join

227

him. "It's hard to understand all that's involved, and sometimes the labels sound harsher than they are—"

"Like real estate fraud?" I say. "Mail and wire fraud. Siphoning investor money, putting it into a personal account. Defrauding investors of more than thirty million dollars over the three-year course of the project? I understand."

Everyone looks at me like someone new has walked in. I'm no longer their perfect girl.

Skip puts the knife down. My mom crosses her legs and looks at her shoes. My heart races.

Sammy is still holding Nicole's legs, looking around while cooing and stomping. He doesn't mind that no one's smiling.

"I didn't know how bad it was going to get," my dad says, his shoulders slumped, childlike.

"You didn't know you were going to get caught." I clench my jaw, refusing to cry. I notice my mom's earrings, little amber tears. She looks like she doesn't know anyone in this room. What now? What will become of us? And when do *we* get to choose what happens to us?

"We know how difficult it's been to be here," my mom says. "All cooped up and out of your element. I'm sorry we had to put you through this."

"Oh my god, it's been fine," I say, pissed at her rudeness.

Nicole keeps her head down. I don't know if she's enjoying the sight of Sammy or treating him like a pet—like I do sometimes at parties when I don't know anyone. I look at the animals, pat their heads.

"We were thinking of you having to face your friends," my

mom says. "You'll be happy to know you don't have to. We won't put you through that. None of us are going back."

"What do you mean? Where are we going?" Jay asks.

"I'm going to a—" My dad looks around, like he's forgotten the words. The truth is he's never used these words, never had to. "I'm going to a facility in Oregon. Our attorneys pushed for the location, since you'll be going to college there. First year's been paid for. We thought all of us may as well relocate."

May as well! As if we're just carefree folks. I can't absorb this. Jay and I look at one another. "What about the rest of my senior year?" Jay asks.

"Since this is your last semester," my mom says, "Ms. Spagnoli thought it unwise for you to transfer."

"Yeah, genius call," he says.

"Unnecessary, I mean. She says you can finish long distance with internet, Skype . . . Most of your assignments are online anyway. You have a three-point-five. They're willing to make it work."

"What about me?" I'm gripping the knife.

"You'll go to school in Eugene," my mom says.

Eugene?

I look down at my phone to see if Brose has texted me back. How many times do we have to swing between forgiveness and what feels like hatred? When will he decide to stop the pendulum, and am I supposed to just bow and submit to the answer? Why is none of it up to me?

"I've spoken to Dean Bennet," my dad says. "He's the dean at Lakewood in Eugene—"

"Wait, his name is Dean, and he's the dean?" I ask.

"And," my dad says, annoyed I've interrupted, "you can finish out your sophomore year. It's a public school, so not a lot of hurdles to this. You'll need to take some class required of all sophomores, but—"

"And right now?" I ask. "In the middle of the year?"

Nicole is holding Sammy under his arms. He stands on her thighs.

"It's a fine school, I've heard," my mom says.

"So we're selling the house?" Jay asks.

My parents look at one another. "Yes," my dad says.

"We have to," my mom says.

"Why?" I ask.

I guess I can already think of the reasons—we need money, or maybe the government or something is going to take our house, or maybe we have to move because our town is spitting us out.

No one bothers to answer me, anyway. The way they're handling all this makes me think that they thought this out long before the ruling.

"Annie, the new school will be a good thing," my mom says. "No one will know who we are."

The words are like a potion. No Mackenzie, no Evergreen, no Eric and pitying or resentful teachers. No relying on a guy and his indecisive pendulum. No guilt from not seeing Cee at school, no castle on the hill reminding me of what I once had. *No one will know who you are.*

A future shines before me. A new start in a new world. *A girl walking confidently down the halls, her virginity gone, her dad on a long business trip. She worked in a restaurant, she's in a long-distance relationship, she's kind of a mystery. Who knows why she moved here in the middle of the year. Did she get kicked out of her old school? For what? Grades, drugs? Let's get to know the new girl . . .*

Nicole, as usual, is having trouble hiding what she feels. She's looking at my parents with disgust, and I wonder what's bothering her most: the fact that we're leaving or the fact that my mom *can* leave and just start up again somewhere else, sweeping the dirty secrets under the rug. She sees my mom as Brose once saw me, or perhaps still does: as someone who lives life without consequences, who doesn't play by the same set of rules. How they could still see us this way, I don't know. How do they not see that we do suffer the consequences? We're not getting away with anything. And yet, I feel judged, and Nicole's judgment means something.

"When do we go?" I ask.

"As soon as possible," my mom says.

The fire cracks and pops. This could be such a nice scene if observed from the outside—the glow from the hearth, the family gathered in companionable silence. It makes me never want to speak again. Words turn beautiful scenes into ugly realities.

Skip breaks our long silence. "Why don't we sit?" he says. "Have some dinner."

I don't bother looking at anyone but him. "I need to be alone," I say to him, though everyone can hear. "I'll eat later." He nods, not seeing if it's okay with my parents. I walk to my room.

Brose finally responds, and I have him meet me in the backyard. I get there through the door in Skip and Nicole's bedroom.

We sit on the picnic bench under a pink and gray sky. I can hear the snowcats grooming the mountain, erasing everyone's marks.

I tell him the plan my parents have made, wanting him to see that things aren't so easy for us either. I look at his profile as he absorbs it all. His eyes look sad, but his mouth holds something bitter.

"Good for you," he says. "Start fresh. No one will know a thing."

I cross my ankles and lean back into the table. "Is that what you want?"

"For you or for myself?"

"You. Do you wish you could do the same?"

He takes his hands out of his pockets, drums them on his thighs. "Not really. I mean, I don't have anything to hide."

"I don't either," I say, and everything falls apart.

That new-girl fantasy and the idea that no one would know who we were felt like a serum, but now it's like a poison. While I'm walking down the halls of my new school, I'm hiding my dad, I'm hiding the real reason why we've moved, why my brother isn't in school. I'm hiding my past, my pride and shame, my mistakes and my strengths. My story. And since I've been here in Breckenridge, I've started to like my story.

Brose looks over at me, then places his hand on my leg. "I'm sorry," he says.

"For what?"

"For not doing the same. Letting you have a blank slate. Start new and all that."

"I'm not asking you to," I say, and then I stand up, which I can tell takes him by surprise. I'm not going to beg.

"I need to get back." I nod to the house. He's flustered, thinking this is it. I'll never see him again. Is this how it ends? "I'll talk to you tomorrow."

"Oh," he says, standing. "Okay."

I rise to tiptoe, hold the back of his neck, and bring him toward me. I kiss him, not really sure what I'm saying by it. It's not a tender kiss. It's more of a statement: *I deserve to kiss you. Because I want to and because I know you do, too.*

29

When I get back to the living room, they're all basically in their same places, with empty and half-empty plates on the coffee table. I'm glad Nicole didn't bother with setting the table. I go to the kitchen, take a bite out of the veggies in the pan, and add salt.

"It would have been nice for you to join us," my mother says.

"I want to finish at Evergreen," I say, my hands flat on the counter. "Not just the year, either. I want to graduate from my school."

Skip clears his throat, then begins to collect everyone's dishes.

"You can't," my mom says. "We can't afford it." She seems confused by her own words—totally perplexed. "And we won't have a home."

"We can afford it," Nicole says. "We have savings. And we have a home."

My mom looks like she's been slapped. She makes a sound that is part laugh, part cough. "You can afford it?" she asks.

Nicole doesn't look as sure. "We've been planning on having kids these past ten years and haven't, so . . . you could say my infertility has saved us money. Plus, we don't have many expenses."

My plan doesn't seem as strong now that, once again, I'd have to take from others. I go back to private school at someone else's expense. "I could keep working and help out," I say. "I could pay you back."

Nicole rolls her eyes, but I wonder if she can truly afford two years.

"It's not like we're livin' large," she says, gesturing to the house. "We actually do quite well and we *save* our money."

My mom looks away, her jaw flexing.

"You don't know what it will be like," my dad says.

"I want to know," I say, and Jay looks at me with what seems like respect.

"Annie, this isn't up for discussion," my mom says.

Nicole looks furious, even though she's lightly bouncing Sammy, making him smile and squeal.

"Here," my mom says. "I'll take him. And please stay out of this. These are family matters."

"Family matters?" Nicole says. "If I recall, we *are* family, remember? If she wants to stay and face things, let her stay. We love having them here. Both of them."

"They've been great," Skip says. He puts the dishes into the sudsy water. "I'd miss them if they were gone." He tags on a quick laugh, but it's so fake. Fake in that he was aiming for lightness, but his voice had a timbre of sadness.

"Well, thank you for having them," my mom says. "Things can go back to normal now. Here, I should feed my son." She stands up and walks toward Nicole.

Nicole's still bouncing Sammy on her leg, but she's focused on some distant thought. "Look," she says. "We're sorry this is happening, but let's take a deep breath and be logical. Annie can stay and at least finish her year. It's worked out, hasn't it?" She looks back at me in the kitchen.

"Yes," I say, and even though our town may not want my parents, it might want me. "It's been great."

I immediately look at my mom, her jaw still tight like a spring. If my parents and I were the same age, would we be friends? Would Jay and Dad hang out? Would I be friends with my mom? I know the answer, and it makes me sad.

"Absolutely not," my mom says. "They will *both* stay with me. And I'm sure they don't want to be separated."

Jay and I make eye contact. He's not going to actually agree, but as always I can read his face. The maggot would miss me.

"We're going to be separated anyway," he says. "I'm pretty much done with Evergreen, but Annie isn't. There's still a lot to look forward to there. Plus, it would be good to be free of my immense shadow."

"You mean ego," I say. "Your immense *ego*."

My mom eyes Nicole. "Could you not bounce him so roughly? Here, I'll—"

"I want to stay," I say. "I'm not better off with you. I've changed. I've grown up." I immediately feel a bit stupid for saying this, and yet it's the easiest way to say what I feel, and I guess I like when people can speak simply.

My dad is hearing me, I can tell. I can see him considering it, allowing his mind to listen. It's a look he's given my brother so many times.

"I have a job," I say while looking at him. "I have new

friends. I have a boyfriend. I want to stay. I haven't done anything wrong."

My mom shoots a look at Nicole, as if these horrible things—
friendship, love, responsibility, confidence—are all her fault.

"Staying is not an option," my mom says.

"Yes, it *is* an option." Nicole glances at Skip for solidarity.
"We can take care of her."

"I'm the person who will decide this," my mom says. "And
please, I'll take Samuel now. He wants me."

He doesn't want her. He's having the time of his life.

"God, Mom," I say. "Just let her hold him. She's not going to
steal him. Or me or Jay. We know you're the real-deal mom. If
both of you just stopped lying for once, everything would be
okay." I couldn't help myself.

My mom glares at Nicole, stands up, and takes her baby.
"How could you?" she says with icy calm.

"How could she what?" Jay asks.

Everyone is silent. I can hear the fire pop like a gunshot. Jay
eyes my mom warily, then me, and I have to look down. It's not
like I revealed anything—my mom just latched on to it—the
secret, the guilt.

"It's okay, Ellen," Nicole says. She widens her eyes and uses
her hands as if to push down the tension, smooth it out.

"He needs to be fed," my mom says. "That's all. And I need to
pump for the sitter tonight."

"We need to meet with the attorneys," my dad says, maybe so
we don't think they're going out for fun after sweeping through
this place.

My mom goes toward the hallway with Sammy and her bag. You'd think, since we're family, she'd be able to feed him here.

"Your mom needs you," my dad says to me. "And she thinks it's best for you to be with her and get a new start."

"I don't want a new start," I say. *I don't want a new last name. I have nothing to hide.* Then I say it out loud. "I have nothing to hide."

My dad looks down, either so sorry or so ashamed.

"I'm staying," I say. "I have a life, I have friends in this town. I have someone I really care about. I'm not worried about how people treat me at school. I don't have real friends there, anyway. But I'm going to."

He clenches his jaw. I see him then as the businessman he once was, the man he could still be, appraising the value and logic of something, the gain, the risk.

"Let me go back to school and face it."

"And you'd be okay commuting?" he asks. "You're happy here?"

"Yes," I say, practically stuttering. I realize that, yes, simply "happy" is what I am, something I've never really been before. I feel fully in my body, if that makes any sense. I feel like I can make my own choices and that I have this custom family I've designed to fit me, and no other version exists. I feel like I'm home.

My dad leans back and looks up at the ceiling.

"Well?" I say.

"I've heard what you have to say," he says, and I know it's best to leave it right here. For now.

My mom comes back out, and I can tell she's been crying. If only she'd just say she's wrecked and devastated.

"Jacob, we need to go," she says, her face hard, emotions all ironed out. She walks out the door.

Skip and Nicole wait outside with my mom, letting my dad say good-bye to us on his own.

"I'm sorry," he says, his voice shaking.

Jay and I exchange nervous looks, having never seen our dad defeated. It makes me feel so unsafe, like I'm bobbing in the middle of a dark sea.

I try to calculate him. Is he 90 percent good and 10 percent bad? Or is there more to it—25 percent greed, 45 percent nurturing father, 5 percent dork funny, 11 percent whiskey, cigars, ice cubes, and boy toys? Make that 25 percent. I just can't do this kind of math.

"I'm sorry," he says again.

"What do you want from us?" Jay asks, and my dad seems confused by the question.

"Just be my son," he says, looking at Jay as if this is so obvious. He looks at me. "Just be my daughter. I need you both. I'm grateful—" He utters a sob that triggers my own tears. "I'd be so grateful for you to still love me. That's all."

His words wallop me in the gut, the head, and the heart. I've never seen him like this before. I've never seen him need anything.

Jay and I look at one another, tearful with fear and maybe relief to be asked for something so clear: help.

Still, neither of us answers, and I know he doesn't expect us to.

My dad hugs Jay before he has time to think about it. Then he hugs me. "I don't know, honey. I don't know."

I'm not sure what he's talking about. Life in general, or my fate specifically. I see my mom outside, and for a moment, I wonder if he has asked the same of her, if he's asked for her to love him, and if so, what was her answer?

30

I eat the dinner they all had without me: a meat loaf made with walnuts, oatmeal, V-8 and Worcestershire, and, well, meat. I sit with Jay on the couch that faces the street and watch Skip-Nic talk to our parents outside.

We drink Bud Light, because why the hell not?

"If you asked to stay, Mom would have said yes," I say. "You always get everything."

"Yes, I get everything," he says. "Things are really swell."

"I mean that Mom trusts you more."

"I'm a guy," he says.

"I know. It sucks."

"Look." Jay points his fork to the window. "Nicole's in smack-down mode. Look at her go."

Nicole is gesturing with her arms and my mom is talking back, but not as her calm self. She's actually getting riled up by whatever Nicole's saying. They're sisters, after all.

"Maybe she's working it out," I say. "Nicole is convincing."

"But it's not up to her," Jay says, and takes a drink. "She's not our mother."

I look over at him, carefully so he doesn't notice. *She is your mother. She may be my mother too.*

"You look like her, though," I say. "Nicole."

Jay watches her yelling, and he touches his nose.

Why can't it be out there in the open? Why can't my mom trust us enough to know who she is? She's our mom and always will be. "Jay?" I say.

"Look, they're leaving." He takes a bite from my plate.

We watch our parents get in the car. My dad looks back at us, and I press my hand to the glass, getting a premonition of our lives to come, something defiantly, solidly between us, clear and strong. I can see the top of Sammy's head, his little blue beanie. The black Mercedes doesn't fit on this street of trucks and vans. Our parents begin to drive off. Skip nods at them, his hands in his pockets, then he puts his arm around Nicole.

Jay knocks on the living room window and waves. "Good-bye."

We watch them go, and I want to sob.

"What were you going to ask me?" he asks.

My plate is balanced on my thighs. "Nothing," I say. "I forgot."

When we were kids, we could never sit next each other without kicking or hitting or annoying each other somehow. We'd always have to be separated. And look at us now, our hands to ourselves.

Nicole and Skip walk toward the house, and we continue to watch them through the glass like they're characters in a movie. They open the door and walk into the room. Nicole seems to deflate when she sees our beers.

"Drinking, boys, what else can you do at your aunt and uncle's? Would you like some crack? Or shall we visit a whorehouse? You have fully proved your mother's point."

She storms off to the bedroom. We hear the door slam.

"Ignore her," Skip says.

"We know," Jay says.

Skip walks up to us, taking both of our beers.

"What did my mom say?" I scoot to the edge of the couch. "Did my dad say anything?"

"He did." Skip takes a sip of a beer. "But . . . no change."

"This makes no sense!" I say. "You have to help me."

"Are you sure you'd even want to stay?" Skip asks. "They're your family."

"So are you."

"We're extended, we're—"

"No you aren't," I say, my voice strong, even though it quivers.

"Annie," he says with a look of disappointment.

"You know this is wrong," I say. "You know it."

Skip blows out his breath. "Your dad is going to talk things over with your mom, okay, but I can't help."

I glare at him.

"Hey," he says, "I'm sorry, but it's not my decision. If I'm ever a parent, no one will override me, and I'll be the one to see things through."

I get up, put my plate in the sink, then go to my room, but after sitting on my bed and fuming, I leave my room, taking my blanket with me. I knock on Nicole's door, then let myself in. She's in bed, watching TV. She pats the comforter, and I get in beside her.

think back to the last time we packed—Sadie lounging on Jay's bed, Jay's ease with our bizarre move, my annoyance with the inconvenience of it all. I feel like I have a different life and, most definitely, a different brother. What's stranger than this, though, is that I don't prefer the original one. It's not that I like what has happened, but knowing what I know now makes it impossible to want things as they once were.

Jay comes to my doorway. "So weird I don't have to go to school."

"Lucky," I say, but don't really feel that way, and I can tell that he doesn't feel it either. We are miles away from lucky. "So weird that I do. At some random school. I'll almost stand out more." I've given up on trying to convince anyone to let me stay here, part of me almost relieved. I get to look brave without having to go through with it.

Skip appears next to Jay. "Um, Annie?" he says.

"Yeah?" I unfold a skirt I can't imagine wearing, toss it in the Goodwill pile.

"You don't need to pack," Skip says. "You can stay."

I drop the shirt I'm folding. I asked, I received. And now I'm flooded with fear, regret, and, and . . . I don't know! A wallop of electricity. Have I asked for the right thing? Is this the right choice? Jay and I exchange looks, and he gives me a congratulatory grin that has a tinge of jealousy or sadness or both.

"You talked to them?" I ask Skip.

"Your mom called," he says. "If you want to finish school at Evergreen, you can. If you don't mind the commute, then . . . yeah. You can stay."

My eyes tear up, though I don't know the source. I just feel unbearably happy and sad. Sappy. Had.

"Thank you!" I say. "I swear I'll contribute. I'll help out. I can work on weekends."

He makes a gesture as if he's swatting a fly.

"I better finish up," Jay says, and Skip gives me a slight smile before leaving. They both seem to know I need a moment to absorb this, and I suppose Jay needs to absorb it too. I immediately lie on my back and stare at the ceiling. Just a few weeks ago, I looked around this room with such contempt, and now it's like a haven.

Jay closes his suitcase, then hauls it off his bed. "I'll take this one out. Here, grab this one."

I take the handle of the smaller suitcase, and we roll out to the hall. Jay stops in front of the picture of Nicole holding him as a baby.

"I've never noticed this one before," he says.

"Really? Jesus, you're as observant as a bag of oats."

Nicole comes out of her room and sees what we're looking

at. In the picture she looks so happy and at ease, laughing at the camera, baby Jay in profile staring up at her.

"You were so cute," she says, and tentatively puts her arm around his shoulder.

"I really was," he says.

She tries to hide her joy and focuses on the picture. "My boy," she sighs.

I look back and forth from them together on the wall to them standing in the hall, and in my mind I take a picture.

"You're a wonderful nephew," she says. "I'd say amazing, but I hate that word."

"Thank you, Aunt Nicole," he says.

He walks down the hall, and she stays where she is, looking at the picture. I take his place next to her. She ruffles my hair. "My girl," she says.

Like that, she claims both of us.

There's more energy in the house as the day goes on. Rickie has come over to help out, music is playing, and there's a kind of joy in the air. You don't realize how much you like something or someone until you're going to leave, and the sadness and gratefulness combine into a strange elixir. I can't quite get my head around Jay and me being separated.

Nicole is all business with her checklist, serious and quick. It's happening so fast. Everyone is moving as if careening down this river, and I feel like I've been swept up and can't put my feet down, can't find a branch to hold on to. Rickie will help me drive—the new plan is to take Jay to Denver, then keep his car for myself, which is—sorry, Nicole—*amazing*.

Nicole walks in through the front door and puts her hands on her hips. "Did you get the laundry?" she asks Jay.

"Got it," he says.

"And your jacket in the coat closet?"

He pats the jacket he's wearing.

"Oh," she says.

Skip walks in from outside. He looks around the house, then crosses his arms. We've run out of things to do.

"The receipt for the shirt that was too small!" Nicole says, as if she's a contestant in a game show.

"On your dresser," he says.

"Okay, then," she says, skeptical. "You're sure you have everything?"

"We can always mail it," Skip says.

"Maybe you should leave something on purpose!" she says, and laughs. "Then you'll have to come back." She looks down and bites her lower lip. "And if the roads are too slick, then I really don't think you guys should be driving right now."

Skip puts his hand on her back to calm her down. The touch immediately makes her burst into tears.

"What? It's dangerous, that's all! The roads! People die! Teen boys especially. I read about it."

She's still crying even though this is half comedic. Rickie's wearing the most ridiculous pink trucker hat that says GUAVA. I don't go to hug Nicole, knowing this is just a passing squall. She'll get it together in a second and will say something bossy or angry. She pulls her shoulders back and sniffs, then raises her chin and takes a huge breath as if trying to crush an anxiety attack.

"Let's go outside," Skip says, as if entertaining guests, welcoming them in instead of seeing them off. I mimic her deep breath, still feeling like I'm in that river, holding on to a rock. Skip opens the door. Here we go.

Rickie puts her arm around me as we walk through the door and greet the sunlight. The street is still, unceremonious.

"This is horrible," I say, watching Jay load the car.

"You can talk to him on the phone," she says.

I look up at her. "It won't be the same."

"Why would we want anything to stay the same?"

I have the odd feeling I am feeling things not all people my age will get to feel, and even if they aren't the best things, I'm glad I have them.

"Well, then," Nicole says. "Let's just get this done."

Skip seems to jump in place and claps his hands, then moves them apart and walks toward Jay. He gives him a big strong hug.

"I miss you already," Skip says, and I can't help it. I start to cry, but the kind of cry you can talk and laugh through. Rickie bumps my hip with her own.

"An onion can make people cry, but there's never been a vegetable that can make people laugh," I say.

"Wow," she says.

Jay walks toward Nicole. Huge inflatable hearts are billowing behind her, the neighbor jumping the gun on Valentine's Day.

Nicole sounds like a cat mewling. Jay laughs. "Is that your crying?"

"Yes," she says.

"Aw," he says, like it's the cutest thing ever. "I've never seen you like this before."

She wipes her eyes. "I know. I have feelings." He gives her a hug.

"You need to wash your hair," she says.

"I will," he says.

"Seriously." She holds him close. "And brush it. Jesus, take care of yourself."

"I will."

"But not too much. Don't be vain. Don't take selfies. Drive when you're sad. Find empty roads and play music real loud. Or watch videos about space. We are so insignificant. We're all going to die."

"Oh my god," he says. "You're so weird. It's not like we're never going to talk again—"

"Since your family's having trouble, don't overcompensate when you get to college," she says. "Just . . . be nice. I mean, 'niceness' is an overrated trait, like the worst is to be described as a 'nice guy.' It basically translates into nondescript and boring. My point is to be kind. Be kind and act from a good place. God, I should take my own advice. I'm not kind at all."

"Be kind," he says, pulling away. "To Skip especially. He worships you."

"I know," she says. "What a weirdo." She wipes the skin underneath her eyes, and I do the same as I look up at the curve of blue, cloudless sky. I lock it all in.

"Ready?" Jay says to me and Rickie.

I turn to Rickie. "I think I want to go with him on my own. That okay?"

"Oh," she says. "Yeah. Of course. You should."

From inside the car, we look at them standing there like a family. I hope, more than anything, that Skip and Nicole have one soon. Rickie looks like she belongs to them. Jay and I must have too. They wave, and I hold up my hand, then look ahead.

"Okay, go," I say, and he goes.

"Saying good-bye," Jay says, driving slowly. "Why is it sad? Makes us remember the good times we've had. Oh, Kermit."

I'm too sad to tell him to shut it. He pulls over at the end of the street.

"What are you doing?"

"You should drive. You need practice." He gets out and I crawl over to his side. May as well. I check my mirrors and adjust the seat, then buckle up. I'm excited. I feel kind of boss in this car. I lower the steering wheel. Jay gets in.

"Weird being on this side." He moves his seat back.

"Okay. Ready?"

"All set." He lengthens his legs and relaxes.

I pull ahead slowly, then brake and start again.

"Look at you," he says. "Doing great. You can go a little faster, though."

I drive out of town, periodically looking at the rearview mirror, which is filled with white mountains. I curve around the lake, feeling like a pioneer in a wagon. They must have seen the exact same views, but then comes the jarring town of Silverthorne with its outlets and fast food. We're one of many cars making its exit. I merge onto I-70, nervous with all the big rigs.

"Use your mirrors," Jay says. I merge, making myself not squeeze my eyes shut.

"You could speed up a little," he says.

"All right, all right."

"Sometimes it's more dangerous to go slow."

I speed up a bit on the straight shot to the tunnel. Other cars zoom past me.

"At least I'm not moving to Kansas," he says.

"Yeah," I say. "But then you'd be closer."

"I'd be going to Oregon anyway."

"I know," I say. "Doesn't really matter."

"Does Brose know you're staying?" he asks, and looks over at me.

"Not yet," I say. "Not sure he'll care."

"Make him care."

I smile slightly, but I don't answer.

We drive by a decayed mining town, which is sort of how I feel about our family. Like we were once a successful, booming community and now we're something you pass by.

"Do you remember Nicole?" I ask. "From when we were little." I no longer have a death grip on the steering wheel.

"Yeah," he says. "I do."

"I don't," I say.

"She came over a lot," Jay says. "I remember sledding with her, or being pulled—remember that? She'd pull us on a sleigh through the woods. Give us gingerbread." He smiles to himself, and I imagine eating gingerbread on a sled with Jay, surrounded by huge evergreens.

"Do you remember that?" he asks.

"I think so," I say. "No."

"Are we okay?" I ask. I drive into the tunnel.

"Looks like it," he says. "You're steady. You haven't crashed. I can see ahead."

32

I pull up to the house, which is right on Cheesman Park. Jay gets out and begins to unload. I'm tired already. I feel like I've been riding a horse all day. I take a light load at first, just wanting to get in and see what's what. I haven't been here in ages; it's one of my parents' properties they'll have to sell. Jay timed our arrival to coordinate with their absence.

I open the door to a pretty bleak place. It doesn't look lived in and smells like library books.

I open the window that overlooks the park. The clouds look strange, like I'm underwater watching waves undulating overhead.

"That's it, then," he says, and looks around, assessing its bleakness.

"That's it."

"You're sure this is what you want?" he asks. "You could start all over, you know."

"I know," I say. "But I don't think I want to."

"You're brave," he says.

"Thanks," I say, knowing he's just shared a lot.

"You'll be fine," he says.

"So will you."

He drags his hand along the couch, and we head back outside.

I sit in the driver's seat with the window down. In my head I snap a picture of him standing there, hands in pockets. Portrait of Jay at seventeen, on his way to college, while I drive back to these strangers that we finally know. I realize I'll most likely never live with him again, and the thought scoops out a hole in me.

"Bye, then," I say.

He squints. "I'll see you later." His ironic smirk falls, and he seems to be taking a picture of me as well.

"All right." I start the car and adjust my mirrors, even though they don't need adjusting. I'm just trying to hide my face, which has contorted into a silent pre-cry. I force myself to be composed before looking out the window again. Jay is checking his phone, and when he looks at me, his eyes are watery. I look down, blinking out tears. Jay has the courtesy to pretend he doesn't notice. He clears his throat.

"So, um, have you ever seen that show *I Didn't Know My Brother Was So Cool*?"

I get myself under control. He gives me time. "Never," I say. "But have you seen *I Didn't Know I Had a Baby-Sized Penis*?"

"Hey, I have seen that!" Jay says. "That's why Brose looked so familiar!"

I honk out a laugh, which catches the attention of a passing jogger. He has blond hair and looks like a popular guy in a teen movie. In fact everyone looks so clean and tidy here. I miss the mountain people. My laugh has brought a huge smile to Jay's face.

I let my foot off the brake. The car crawls ahead. A pair of ducks scrape the sky, wings out, low bellies. He walks alongside me.

"Bye, Annie," he says.

I smile, not trusting my voice. I can feel my mouth quiver. He stops walking, letting me go, and when I've passed him, I sob quickly, like a hiccup, then continue to cry, but soundlessly, peacefully.

I look at him in the rearview mirror. He holds up his hand, then turns and walks to the house. The clouds look like they've been raked.

33

I missed the first few days of school because of reenrollment issues and, well, because I can. I was planning on going the second day, but Nicole took one look at me Thursday morning, the day after I brought Jay to Denver, and said, "No way."

I'm not sure what she saw. Someone in shock or in mourning. Someone unprepared. Maybe she saw me as something not quite solidified, something still forming, which is how I felt.

"No way."

I zombie-walked back to my room then, half an hour later, came back out. She looked up, was about to ask where I was going, I'm sure, but saw I was in my snowboard gear.

"Have fun," she said, and I headed out to ride.

Now it's Friday, and I'm on my third day missing school. It's also my third day following her original itinerary: I've gone to the museum, I've done the sleigh ride, I've gone tubing, which was really fun. I actually laughed out loud, and now I'm doing something not on her itinerary.

I walk in the side door of Steak and Rib, put my hair up, tie an apron on, and shock the hell out of Brose, who is sharpening his favorite Richmond knives.

"Hey," I say. He looks so good. I have an urge to push myself against him, his rough jeans that always have a slight smell of firewood.

"Hey," he says. "What are you doing here?"

It's then that I realize that not only did he think I had left, but he was fine without me saying good-bye. My bravado weakens.

"I live here now," I say. "I'm staying."

He continues sharpening the blade, the sounds making me feel jolted. He doesn't ask me any questions, the ones I've prepared answers for.

"I'm staying at my school, toughing it out."

"Toughing it out at your private school?" He smirks. "That's great you can stay."

"Skip and Nicole are helping . . ." I realize how spoiled I sound, even though I don't feel that way. "And I'm going to work when I can."

I want to run away; I feel ridiculous with this apron on, like I've gotten a role I didn't earn. Work when I can. Take it or leave it.

There's no one else here. I know he comes earlier to log more hours, do extra work cleaning the bar and answering phones.

"I didn't want to run away or start fresh," I say. "I know you don't think it's a big deal, but my cushy private school isn't going to be very friendly, and I'm staying here because I like it. I feel myself here. I love what I have here."

I look down, take my hair out. I don't want to be in this kitchen, can't play this part.

"Anyway," I say, "I'll be around. Get used to it. This is my town, too, and I'm not going to be giving these slow-clap speeches every time we meet."

He looks up, and his mouth twists into a reluctant grin.

I take off my apron. On my way out I hear him clapping, slowly.

EPILOGUE

They used to look at me and then they stopped and now they look again. My first week back was awkward, and the whole time it felt like I was onstage performing poorly. My audience was uncomfortable, always seemed to be either snickering or pitying me. Even teachers treated me gently, like I could break. Jay's absence, though never talked about, filled the halls, almost like something you could smell or taste.

The following weeks were even harder. People grew more comfortable asking me questions, and the questions were a performance for others.

"What's it like having a dad in jail?" Bree asked in PE, surrounded by her squad. She'd never have had the balls to ask me alone.

"It's like this," I said, bouncing my ball hard. "I go to school. I go home."

"But not home," she says, her eyes laughing, needing the attention, confirmation from others. "I heard the place you're staying in is nothing like your old place."

"Nope," I said. "Anyway. You should call me since you're so interested. I can give you all the details of what it's like to have a dad in jail. I've got loads to tell you. Call me!" I made the cute little thumb-pinkie call-me sign, then dribbled my ass out of there. She hasn't talked to me since.

There were people like Joffrey, who didn't think twice about talking to me, asking me about Jay. There were also people like Eric and Sadie, who seemed embarrassed by their own actions of abandoning a friend in need.

The commute—air, music, mountains, solitude—ended up not being a burden, but a refuge, a relief.

By the middle of the second month, the looks sort of stopped. People were busy with their own issues: school, sports, who liked who, their own neglectful/messed-up/forgetful/overly involved/fill-in-the-blank parents.

And now? Almost two months later, they've begun to look again.

What's up, Annie?

Did you finish your lab?

Do you want to come by with Ash later?

And even: *How's your mom and dad doing? Does Jay like Eugene?*

Normal. Or, I guess not, because this isn't normal. With a different version of myself in place—confident but not smug, carefree but dependable, determined but light—there's a new normal. It's one that I like a lot.

Though sometimes, not so much. When your boyfriend's dad is putting together a civil suit against your father, who's already in jail, that's not so great.

Knowing your mom went from a family of five, living in a palatial mountaintop home, to a family of three, living in a two-bedroom rental—that's not the best new normal I can think of.

Money can't buy happiness? That may be true. But not having it anymore makes me understand that it can buy you a kind of effortlessness. I didn't think about saying no to something because I couldn't afford it—like not going to eat somewhere, see a show, shop, or have the choice to do nothing. I have to work now—not just at the restaurant to help out, but at being a good household member, at proving myself to Brose, to people at school. I have to work at managing my time. I have to work on myself because that's who I'm going to have to depend on.

Still, despite it all, I smile more than I did before, and if you made a list comparing what I had before to what I have now, that seems remarkable.

I'm doing so now—smiling—as I walk on the vast green field at sunset. The sky is pink and blue, and the mountain range is far in the distance, white swells on the horizon. Even though the mountains are far away, they're still the focal point. This all seems to spill out from them.

I see Ash walking toward me, my new friend who's such a doofus, but she has these long model limbs and a stunning face. She's a junior, and I knew her from a distance as one of the popular, fancy girls. On my first day back, she sat next to me in AP English—or tried to, since she missed her chair. We both lost our shit laughing and have been friends ever since. I'm sleeping at her house this Thursday and Friday so I can skip a drive and then have weekend time with people from school. She gestures that she'll meet me in the parking lot.

I give a thumbs-up, then answer a call from Nicole.

"Hey," I say. "I'm exercising. Kind of."

"Cool," she says. "But you don't sound out of breath."

I start to pant until she tells me to cut it out. "What's up?" I ask.

"Not much," she says. "Skip's looking at motorcycles on his laptop. I wish he'd read a book. Learn about stocks or something."

She stops talking, and I hear water trickling. "Oh my god, are you peeing?"

"Sorry," she says, and then I hear a flush. "So you're sure Ash's parents are okay with you staying until Sunday?"

"Yeah, I told you."

"Remember tonight's a school night."

"I know, I—"

"And tomorrow night, don't go crazy or anything. Don't drink and drive, and don't just leap into things. You don't want boys to recognize you from the back of your head."

"Jeez," I say. "You should really write a book of advice for teens."

"Oh my god!" she says.

"What?" I'm almost to the car, and I stop walking. "Are you okay? Nicole?"

I hear a door close. "I'm here," she says.

"Why are you whispering?"

"I don't know," she whispers. "When you heard me peeing, I was peeing on a test."

My throat sort of constricts. "And?"

"And it's positive. And my boobs hurt so I thought maybe, but sometimes they hurt before my period so I didn't know if it was just that or—"

"It's positive," I say, trying to calm her.

"Yes," she says. "Yes."

I imagine her in the bathroom holding the test, maybe

looking at her reflection as if she's now someone slightly changed, a translation. Our family, ever changing. I close my eyes, relishing this feeling of being so happy for something that doesn't have to do with me.

I stop walking in the field and watch the descending sun. "Go tell Skip that you want to see what's in the shed," I say.

"Why?" she says. "That sounds creepy."

"It's not," I say. "It's good. Say you're ready. Tell him I told you to ask. Trust me."

"Okay," she says.

My eyes water. I wish Brose was here. "I'm going to let you go now. Promise me you'll ask him."

"Okay," she says. "Bye."

"Bye," I say, my voice breaking.

I continue to walk, because I'm too excited to stay still. I have a huge smile on my face, imagining them walking toward the shed, Skip about to reveal the gift he made with his own hands. I'm witnessing the beginnings of a mother and father.

I'm about to call Brose, needing to share the news, but realize it's Jay I need to call, who I want to call.

"Hey," he says.

"Nicole just took a test, and it's positive," I blurt out. "And I told her to have Skip show her the shed."

"Cool," Jay says, and I hear the smile in his voice. "So they're walking out there now?"

"I think so. I'm at school."

"How's it going?" he asks.

"Good," I say. "Really good. You?"

"Same," he says. "Really good." I hear the hesitation and

recognize it. The "good" is surprising to both of us, accompanied by a feeling of guilt. We are good. We're going to be okay.

"You think they're looking at it now?" he asks.

I look to the mountains. "I wish I was there!"

"She's sobbing, I bet," he says, matter-of-fact, and I start to tear up.

"I bet they're just holding each other," I say.

"But then she'll stop, pretend it's not a big deal."

"That it probably won't work," I say.

He laughs. "Skip will just grin," Jay says. "That dumb smile that takes up his whole face."

"Yeah," I say. "He's so proud of that crib. She better be nice about it."

I can see them so clearly in that sweet yard. The air a little colder, the sky a little darker. I can see Jay in Oregon. My parents, my baby brother. Maybe they're okay, too. I guess when you have no choice, you just have to be. You design your family with what you have. It's sort of like making your own clothes—you have some materials, then you create a pattern and make it fit, adjusting, altering, sometimes cutting and throwing away. In the end it will come together, perfectly imperfect.

"Thanks for calling," Jay says.

"Of course."

I want so badly to tell my brother that I love him. I miss him. I never will, but he'll always know. I stay on the phone, as if it's connecting us, all of us, and even though I'm alone at this moment, I feel held.

ACKNOWLEDGMENTS

As always, thank you to Kim Witherspoon and David Forrer—how I love having you on my side—and thank you to Ari Lewin for your guidance. Jim Burke, producer and friend extraordinaire: thank you for encouraging me to write a screenplay. I tried, stopped, and then turned it into this book.